Raspberry House
Blues

Raspberry House Blues

Linda Holeman

Tundra Books

Published in Canada by Tundra Books,
McClelland & Stewart Young Readers,
481 University Avenue, Toronto, Ontario M5G 2E9

Published in the United States by
Tundra Books of Northern New York,
P.O. Box 1030, Plattsburgh, New York 12901

Library of Congress Control Number: 00-131577

Canadian Cataloguing in Publication Data

Holeman, Linda, date
    Raspberry house blues
ISBN 0-88776-493-2
I. Title.

PS8565.06225 R37 2000   jC813'.54   C00-930682-X
PZ7.H64Ra 2000

We acknowledge the support of the Canada Council for the Arts
and the Ontario Arts Council for our publishing program.

We acknowledge the financial support of the Government of
Canada through the Book Publishing Industry Development
Program for our publishing activities.

Design by Terri-Anne Fong

Printed and bound in Canada

1 2 3 4 5 6   05 04 03 02 01 00

For my daughter Brenna,
who dyed her hair red while
I was dreaming about Poppy

"Keep a green tree in your heart,
and perhaps the singing bird will come."

Chinese Proverb

ONE

I knew something was wrong by the music coming from the open kitchen window. Explosive music – lots of violins wailing out a crazed Russian or Polish mazurka – something that can only be described as a gypsy campfire thing. My mother likes music by Barry Manilow or Neil Diamond, and never loud.

"Stupid. Stupid, stupid. I hate these," I said, unbuckling my rollerblades and throwing them onto the grass. They were secondhand, scratched and dull. The left skate always seemed wobbly, and the top clasp on the right one didn't work. In less than a month – by the end of June – I would have enough money saved for a new pair. Mom had given these used ones to me for Christmas, apologizing. I said it was okay, but it wasn't, and she knew it. The skates weren't okay, and she wasn't okay.

I sat on the grass for a minute, letting the cool early-evening breeze dry the sweat off my arms and legs. The gentle wind carried the faintest smell of the ocean.

Leaving my skates on the grass, I opened the back door and was nearly knocked over by the blasting beat from the radio. The noise was bad enough, but what was even worse was that my mother was dancing, twirling through the kitchen, clapping her hands; her cheeks bright with two circles of pink, like a baby whose teeth are coming in. My mother's cheeks are rarely pink without the aid of a brisk wind. It took me a few seconds to realize that it was because she was having fun, even though she looked ridiculous. You really can't twirl in stretchy old-lady jeans.

I stood watching her, and watching Marcus – her boyfriend, who was also watching her – clap his hands in time with hers. Marcus did not have pink spots on his cheeks. His whole face was a dark red, sort of splotchy. He needed a haircut, his brown and gray streaked hair messy in a starving-artist kind of way.

"I'm thinking rum and coke, Denise," Marcus yelled, above the music.

"Make mine white wine," my mom yelled back, whirling even faster. "Wine today, next month – ouzo!"

Something heavy lurched in my stomach.

Marcus went toward the bottles on the counter. As my mother twirled by, he caught her around the waist and made this very pathetic attempt at swaying with her. His jeans hung too low, sagging in the bottom, with a kind of white glow that means they're on the verge of wearing through. Marcus is very tall and what I consider flabby. Mom says he's big-boned, with genetically poor muscle tone.

Neither of them had spotted me. *Am I a chameleon to blend in so smoothly, to go so unnoticed in my own home?*

Marcus' hands slid further around my mother's middle. She closed her eyes, in ecstasy, I imagined.

I'll go out and come home later, I thought. I didn't want to be seeing any of this – my mother looking so . . . I don't know . . . wanton, to use a romance novel word.

"Marcus," I'm sure I heard my mother murmur, although the music was too loud to hear a murmur. If she were wearing what is called a bodice, as opposed to her sensible tangerine turtleneck, I'm sure Marcus would be ripping it open right now.

Please let me die.

Before I could turn and run, the music mercifully ended and was replaced by a soothing radio voice. In the relative quiet, I was afraid to move.

My mother laughed, a strange throaty laugh, and opened her eyes. Even with the fading evening light, I could see that her eyes were dreamy and unfocused. She laughed a second time, brushing her hair away from her flushed cheeks with both hands and looking up into Marcus' face. I was so afraid that she'd do something unbelievable, like kiss him right in front of me, that I shouted – "Mom!" – way too loud, surprising even myself.

"Oh. Poppy," she said, putting her hands onto Marcus', and pushing herself away from him. Slowly. *Reluctantly?* "What are you doing here?" Her eyes immediately lost their dreaminess and hardened into a narrow gaze, the one reserved for me and me alone. She walked briskly to the other side of the kitchen and switched off the radio.

The room was too hot, too quiet, Marcus' face too red.

"Gee, Mom, perhaps you've forgotten. I live here."

"Well. We – I – wasn't expecting you for a while yet. We were celebrating."

"That's obvious," I said, getting a clean glass from the dishwasher and pouring myself some cola from the big no-name bottle on the counter. It was warm and had lost its fizz. I drank it anyway.

"Marcus just found out he got a travel grant. A big one."

"Hello, poppet," Marcus said, clearing his throat.

"It's Poppy," I said.

I could hear my mother's breath whistling over her bottom lip in irritation. "Poppet is a Middle English term of endearment. A poppet is a dainty person, an endearing child. So it's a compliment, Marcus calling you that."

Marcus is a writer. Actually, a poet, although he writes travel articles for money. Poetry doesn't bring in much money, Marcus has repeatedly said, but that fact is immaterial since it opens your soul. Marcus has been working really hard on teaching my mother to open her soul, to go with the ebb and flow of her psyche. This explains the twirling in the kitchen, the gypsy music, perhaps even the wine. It does not explain what "ooh-zoh" is. Nor does it explain the way I feel about her now.

"I'm not an endearing child," I said, opening the fridge in the hope that there would be something interesting inside. A leftover pork chop mummified in Saran Wrap, three flavors of yogurt, a jar of gherkins and one of olives, as well as all the usual fridge standards – milk and juice, margarine, eggs. "I'm hardly dainty," I went on, closing the door. "And what I just had to witness wasn't a discussion."

"Now, don't start anything," my mother said. She gave Marcus the look I hated. The one that said, well, what can you do?

I took another mouthful of flat cola, then, leaving the half-full glass on the counter, walked past my mother and Marcus. "The dainty poppet will now go to her sweet little poppet room, where she can hopefully get some studying done."

"Poppy," my mother said. "Could you wait for just a minute? We – I – wanted to talk to you about something. Please?" Her eyes were suddenly too bright.

"No," I said. "I have exams starting next week. And could you keep the music down?"

"Poppy!" Now she was shouting. "Don't you walk away when I'm talking to you. Do you hear me?" She grabbed the top of my arm, but I yanked away from her, walking down the hall to my room and slamming the door. It felt good to hear the crash and feel the shudder in the walls, and I waited, listening for more of my mother's yelling, but there was only silence after the echo of the slam faded.

My biology text and notes were sitting in a neat pile on my desk. Sharpened pencils and a stack of blank paper sat beside them. Ignoring it all, I opened the bottom desk drawer and took out my *M* Book, then sat on the bed and started to flip through the pages, glancing up at the full-length mirror on the back of my door every now and then, studying the pictures I'd cut out of magazines and comparing them to what I saw in the mirror. The *M* Book always made me feel better.

I heard the sound of Marcus' motorcycle starting up, and within thirty seconds my door burst open.

"How could you be so rude?" Mom yelled, her hand gripping the doorknob. "How, Poppy? We wanted to talk to you about something, something important, and you couldn't even give us the time of day. Just strolled off as if you were royalty. As if we were beneath you."

I raised my eyebrows. "You said it; I didn't." I waited one pulse beat. "I heard lover boy leave."

My mother's eyes glanced at the book on my lap, and her nostrils tightened. "Of course. Do you expect him to stay with you acting up, playing the drama queen for all you're worth? What's wrong with you? Why are you trying to wreck what little life I have?"

"Me? Wreck your life? How do you think I feel, seeing you with your hands all over Marcus? It's disgusting."

"We were dancing, Poppy. Dancing. Aren't I allowed to dance?"

I shrugged, picking at one corner of the page, then slowly ran my hand over the glossy image. It calmed me to touch these pictures I'd glued into the scrapbook. Pictures of women who looked like *she* might. . . .

"Are you still fussing with that book?" Even though her voice was quieter now, the way Mom said "that book" sounded as if her mouth were full of sand.

I let a smile play on my lips, even though I didn't feel like smiling, and kept my hand on the page in front of me. Some of the pictures were of actresses, some models. All of them were of tall women with red hair. "So what do you want? Apart from telling me how rude I am?"

"Poppy," my mother said, shaking her head, the two vertical lines between her eyebrows growing deeper. She stared at me, and then down at the book, her mouth making fishy circles as if she was trying to say something, but nothing came out.

I stood – back straight, chin high – thinking Audrey Hepburn. "If you don't mind," I said, closing the scrapbook and hugging it to my chest, "I'm rather busy." I thought the English accent worked well. I pushed at the door with my foot, and my mother's hand dropped away from the doorknob. She stepped back into the hall.

One more small shove with my foot and the door swung closed. I pushed in the little button on the knob, and the door locked with a satisfying click. "Perhaps some other time," I said to myself in the mirror, admiring the way I could see the line of my cheekbone if I turned my head just so. Then, a little louder, "Perhaps some other time, *Mother*."

I knew that the way I said "Mother" hurt her, and that felt good. I was safe on this side of the door, unable to see her face. "You obviously don't have time for me, anyway," I said through the wood. "You'd prefer it if I wasn't here. Then you could do whatever you damn well please. I'll bet you ask yourself every day what made you want me in the first place."

"Stop it," my mother said. "Just stop it." Her voice grew shrill. "Stop feeling sorry for yourself."

"I'm not feeling sorry for myself," I yelled back. "And you stop telling me how to feel – what to think and do." I was really into it now, my mouth right up against the door. "Who do you think you are, anyway?"

I thought she'd left. The silence stretched, and I realized I felt even more empty than usual, like all the substance had been sucked out of my body. I backed up slowly, until I felt the edge of my bed behind my knees, and sat down hard, the *M* Book cradled against me.

But she was still there. "I'm your mother," came her voice, softly, through the door.

I lowered the book to my lap. "No, you're not," I called, not loudly, but loud enough for her to hear. "No, you're not," I repeated. "You're not my real mother. And you never will be."

And then I waited, but there was nothing more – no voice, no sound of footsteps, nothing – until eventually I became aware of the familiar sound of soft Vancouver rain outside my window, and I realized that my room was in darkness.

I wondered if it was raining in Winnipeg, where my real mother had lived, and maybe still lived. I had been born in Winnipeg, and she had given me up for adoption there. I was tall, and had red hair. I'm sure she was tall, and had red hair, too.

Is she listening to the rain in Winnipeg, and thinking about me?

TWO

The next day after school, she told me about her plans to leave while we were at the compost heap in the backyard.

"Dump it there," Mom said, and I emptied the pail of vegetable parings and eggshells and coffee grounds she'd called for me to bring out from under the kitchen sink.

"Put down the pail and listen. What I wanted to tell you last night, Poppy, is that I'm going away. With Marcus." Just like that. No warning, nothing. Just "I'm going away."

Two can play that game. "Fine," I said. *What about me?* "When?"

"As soon as you're done exams and I finish up at school. My last class is June 15." My mother teaches adult education at the community college. "So when are you finished?"

"June 17."

"Okay. I'll tell Marcus, and he can book our flights."

I swung the empty pail against my leg while my mother worked the heap, forking the smelly gunk over and under.

"To Greece," she said, as if I'd asked where she was going. I hadn't.

"Greece? Greece, as in . . . Greece?" *What about me?*

"I told you last night that Marcus got a travel grant because he's working on a collection of poems to do with some of the ruins on the island of Crete. He's asked me to go with him, and I said yes. We're both borrowing a little extra money." She jabbed the pitchfork into the pile one more time.

"You always told me you wouldn't borrow unless it was an emergency."

"Maybe it *is* an emergency, Poppy. I'm forty-seven, and I've hardly been anywhere except Winnipeg and here. Maybe it's time I have a chance to do something I really want to do, instead of what I have to do." She still hadn't looked at me.

"And what about me?" I finally said.

"No problem. I've spoken to Auntie Jan, and she says it's fine for you to stay with her. You can still do everything that you planned for the summer − go to work, take the acting class you signed up for, hang out with your friends. It's no problem," she repeated, a little too loudly, although maybe it was the exertion of digging that made her words come out in short, hard jabs.

"No problem? No problem for who? For *whom*, Mother? Did you ever think it might be a problem for me? That I don't *want* to stay with Jan and her bratty kids? And she's not my aunt; she's just your friend. For how long? How long would I have to stay there?"

Mom finally looked at me, having to look up because she's really small – barely five feet – but her eyes got all busy, like they possessed some kind of secret pond life. A swarm of tiny black gnats flew up around her face, and she waved them away, but again, she didn't answer the question.

"It depends on how long our money holds out. And you'll be fine at Jan's." She snicked her lips together. "Don't look at me like that. Just grow up, Poppy. You keep telling me how I don't give you enough space, enough freedom. So now I'm giving it to you. You'll be free of me for a while, Poppy. Your wish has come true."

"You really expect me to spend my summer at Jan's?" I said again, my voice loud, rumbly. I was trying hard to take this in. The smell from the compost was making me feel shaky and weird.

My mother straightened up, her right hand on the small of her back, her left holding the pitchfork. Her face was still, her voice low. "Just cut the crap, Poppy. I'm sick of your melodrama. Save it for the stage. Don't you think of anyone except yourself? It's not going to hurt you to stay with Jan for a bit. Wouldn't you say I should have a chance to do something that I want, for once? Why does life have to revolve around what you want?"

The thudding of my heart was interfering with my audio. I had to talk even louder to hear myself. "So you're just going to abandon me?"

She glanced toward the neighbor's yard, then looked back at me. "*Shhh*," she hissed. "Stop shouting. Everything has to be such a big production with you, doesn't it?" Her fingers massaged her lower spine, and her forehead looked sweaty for such a cool day. But she had been working pretty hard with the pitchfork. She drove the fork into the putrid pile again, grunting with the effort.

She can't stop me that easily. "Some mother you are."

A tiny tic pulled at one side of her mouth.

I stood tall, an invisible string stretching from the top of my head to the telephone cable above us. I took a deep breath. "But then you aren't a real mother," I said, quietly, but making my voice hard. Severe.

Mom flinched as I said those last two words for the second time in two days. I saw the flinches. Real – *flinch* – mother – *flinch*. The same feeling of power that I had when I heard laughter from the audience in the darkness beyond the stage lights of the gym at school filled me now.

"You're just a pretend mother. You don't have a clue."

"And all those pictures you keep cutting out, filling that Mother Book or whatever you call it, you think those are real mothers?"

"All I know is that there's someone out there who does care, more than you'll ever know how. Because you aren't capable of real mother love."

She turned her head away, and I saw a minuscule tremor in the handle of the pitchfork before she had a chance to grip it with her right hand. Her denim shirt strained across the back as she lifted another forkful, and I left her there, with the softening eggshells and rotting vegetables and sweet-sour decaying grass. I thought I would continue to feel powerful as I walked away from her, but the image of her small hard-working back and shoulders wouldn't leave, and instead, my throat ached with something unfamiliar and acidy.

I stayed in my room the rest of the afternoon and into the evening, ignoring the rich meaty smell of supper cooking, trying to find comfort in my *M* Book, studying the faces of women that I imagined my real mother might look like – the mother who gave me up for adoption. Usually looking through the book could start to close up the empty feeling that I've had for the last few years, ever since Mom and I stopped getting along.

But this time even the book didn't work.

🌳

"Dad? Dad, it's me."

"Poppy? What's wrong? Why are you whispering?"

"I'm not. I'm just talking quietly. Listen, I'm coming to Winnipeg, okay?"

"What? When? You're coming here? Why?"

Not exactly the response I'd been hoping for, but it would have to do.

"Look, I just need to come there for a while. I have to do something. Something I've been thinking about for a long time." *I'm coming to Winnipeg to look for my real mother.*

"Let me talk to your mother."

"She's not here. I'm at her friend Jan's house right now."

"Where is she?"

"It's a long story, Dad. I'll fill you in when I get there. I just need to let you know I'm coming tomorrow, so you can meet me at the airport. The only trouble is, I have to fly standby, so I'm not sure when I'll get there. But I'll call you when I know what flight I'm on."

"Tomorrow?" There was a little coughing sound. "Did you say tomorrow?"

"Yeah."

"I think I need to talk to Denise about this."

"I told you, Dad, you can't. She's gone. She took off, all the way to Greece."

"Greece? As in . . ." His voice drifted.

"Yeah. As in Greece. So I'll call you tomorrow, okay?" I could hear a little kid crying somewhere in the background, and a woman's voice, low and comforting. The crying stopped.

"I guess so," Dad said, in his usual stunned way.

"It'll be fine, Dad. Trust me." I gave a little laugh, but Dad didn't join in.

"I should speak to Calypso about this," he said.

"Whatever. See you tomorrow," I said, and hung up before he could ask any more questions, or hem and haw about anything else.

Poor old Dad. What a joke.

THREE

"Hi. Dad! Dad, over here. It's me."

Dad's eyes widened. "Oh. Hi, hi Poppy. Yeah, yeah, I knew it was you. It's just that you're . . . taller. Way taller."

"No kidding," I said. "I guess I grew a few inches, or seven, in the last three years."

"And with the sunglasses on. . . ."

I didn't take them off.

"Isn't your hair . . ." He couldn't seem to find the right word. "Shorter? But still red. Is it darker? It looks darker than I remember. I was always glad you had the dark red hair, and dark eyes." He was babbling, clearing his throat, blinking too fast. "The fair kind of redhead always has more trouble with their skin."

I nodded.

Dad was still fixated on my hair. "So, is it hard to make your hair do that? Do you use gel? It *is* darker, isn't it?" He shot off the three questions like he didn't really expect answers, but I gave them to him anyway.

"Nope. Yeah. Nope."

He cleared his throat again, now rubbing his hands together briskly, a busy fly. I could hear the dry scraping of his palms. "Well . . . you've changed since I saw you last. That's for sure."

"Like I said, it's been three years."

"Yeah. Well," he said, for the second time, and stopped rubbing his hands. He put his right one out, and up, like he didn't know whether to place it on my shoulder or hug me or shake my hand. "Sorry about that. But with Calypso, and then the baby, and the move back up to Canada and everything. . . ." His hand hung in front of me. I saw that the pads of his fingers were calloused, just like I remembered them. He was still playing his guitar, then. Still imagining he was some great blues player.

I made it easy for him, stepping away from his hand and heading toward the luggage conveyor belt. "I've got a huge gym bag and a big box," I said, over my shoulder. He was following me. "There's a lot."

"Are you staying long?" His voice seemed to have gone up a tone.

I tried for nonchalant. "Not sure. We'll see. It depends how it goes." I thought of IT in capital letters.

"Flight okay?"

"It was okay."

❦

It had been a long day; I'd waited at the airport since early morning to finally get a seat on a late-afternoon flight on standby. After I'd phoned Dad yesterday, I'd taken all my money out of my bank account, everything I'd saved from working at Divine Blue all year — except for what I'd spent on new clothes, at twenty percent off — and then got a refund on my acting class registration fee. It was enough for my flight, and enough left over that I didn't feel broke.

Before I'd left Jan's I'd written a note telling her not to worry, that I'd worked it all out with my dad to stay with him instead. I even left his phone number. My friend Kate borrowed her brother's car and she and Danielle drove me to the airport.

"I can't believe you're doing this," Danielle had said. "It's so cool. Just leaving like this."

"I thought Kieran might have come," Kate said, craning her neck to look around the drop-off area at the airport.

"We said good-bye on the phone last night." I was glad neither of them were looking at me as I told the lie. I had left three messages for Kieran over the last two days, telling him I was leaving Vancouver, asking him to call me at Jan's, but he hadn't returned any of them. It's not like we were officially going out, but he could have at least made an effort.

I'd flown only once before, a school trip down to Seattle, but this three-hour flight was just as uneventful. I figured out the best way to do it was the "I vant to be alone" thing, and not talk to anyone, just keep my eyes fixed on my magazines. I'd even kept my sunglasses on the whole time. They were cat's-eye black plastic, studded with diamondy glass chips; I'd bought them at Complete Vintage.

I kept up the role coming down the escalator. *Don't look left or right, but keep your eyes, invisible to the prying public, fixed on an unknown and distant horizon. Chin high, arms crossed loosely, the haughty yet casual approach. You are a world-famous heiress, traveling incognito, avoiding recognition by any possible reporters.*

I'd spotted Dad right away, and it was clear that he hadn't recognized me, no matter how hard he tried to pretend.

He hadn't changed at all – same too-long straggly dark blond hair and unstylish handlebar mustache. Probably different faded jeans and cowboy boots than he wore in the few pictures I had of him, but they looked the same. His white T-shirt was all wrinkly, but at least it was clean. As I got closer I could see a lot more creases fanning out from his eyes than the last time I saw him, just before I turned thirteen. I'd always thought of him as tall, compared to Mom. Now he and I were almost the same height.

Since that last time, when he came up from California to visit me, he'd been pretty busy with his new family – that's what Mom told me – and there had only been birthday and Christmas cards. Always with cash. There might be a ten or a twenty. One year there were just five crinkled one dollar bills. Mom has always said that my father is the kind of guy who will never have money.

I was about five when Dad left us. He'd moved from our house in Vancouver over to Vancouver Island, staying up in Nanaimo for a while. Then he'd migrated down to Victoria, then further south, into the States, to Seattle. He'd eventually worked his way down the coast until he ended up in California. He had to keep coming back to Canada because he couldn't get a green card to actually live there. For that you have to have a real job. My dad gave up his real job (he was the manager of a large flooring company that sold tiles and sheet flooring and carpeting) and, it seems to me, his real life as Mr. Ordinary Family Man when he left Mom and me. He gave away his suits and ties and, from that time on, let his hair grow, and just drifted around, playing his old guitar, Brownie, and picking up odd jobs to make enough to support himself. Until I was thirteen, he had come back to Vancouver to see me a couple of times a year at least. He never had enough money to do much, but we'd just hang out, going to Stanley Park or taking the cable car up Grouse Mountain – simple stuff. On that last visit he'd taken me to a coffee shop and ordered me a coffee – an Arabian Mocha Java – and I was hooked.

Maybe he had girlfriends or relationships, but I never heard about anyone. Until Calypso.

🌳

"So is this it? The whole airport?" I asked, looking around.

"Well, there's more down that way," Dad said, vaguely waving behind him.

"It's so small compared to the Vancouver airport."

"You're not in Kansas anymore, Dorothy," he said.

"Very funny." At least he remembered. I'd had my first speaking role in a play that last time he'd come to Vancouver, and he'd watched it. I'd played the Tin Man in *The Wizard of Oz*.

"So, do you still have Brownie?" I asked, for something to say when the silence got uncomfortable.

"Yup. Got a few paying gigs over the winter."

We stared at the motionless luggage belt. Dad kept clearing his throat, like he was going to say something, but nothing came out for a while.

"That woman – Jan – already phoned," he finally said. "I don't know how she got our number, but she called, pretty worried. She doesn't know what she's going to tell your mom."

"What kind of car do you have now?" I asked, not wanting to think about that. "Do you still have the El Camino?" I had liked the old car-truck thing Dad used to drive. "I got my license last month, right after my six-teenth birthday."

He cleared his throat one more time. "No."

"So what do you have?"

"I use the van during working hours. The van from work. I deliver for Karpet King." He squinted at the luggage belt. Still nothing. "Calypso and I pretty much rely on our feet the rest of the time," he said.

"Feet? You don't have your own car?"

"Not right now. The environment, and all that." His eyes flicked to one side. "Calypso would rather not pollute the air any more than necessary. Like I said, I can use the van on the days I work."

"No car?" I repeated, unnecessarily.

"Nope. But I've got good news."

"You're going to buy a car tomorrow?"

He blinked, then frowned, as if he wasn't sure whether I was being sarcastic or not. I was. "No. But I asked around at work this morning, and a buddy gave me a used bike for you. It's a three-speed."

A three-speed. Maybe it has a banana seat and colored streamers on the handlebars, like the last used bike he bought me when I was five. Hopefully this one doesn't have training wheels. "Oh, good," I said, not even trying to keep the sarcasm out of my voice this time. He didn't appear to notice.

"I was thinking I might pick up some paint; give it a once-over and spruce it up."

As I opened my mouth to tell him not to bother, that I wouldn't be reduced to riding someone's cast-off bike, there was a loud buzz and, with a jerk, the luggage belt started moving.

"Here they come," Dad said, smiling in a kind of relieved way, staring at the belt. "Here they come," he repeated, and we stood there, side by side, watching the luggage tumble out and around as if it were the most fascinating sight in the world.

🌳

"You won't remember anything of Winnipeg," Dad said, as we drove down a quiet street. "You were a baby when we moved out West. So, welcome to Wormwood."

"What?"

"Wormwood. It's a joke," Dad said. "This is really the Wolseley area, but I call it Wormwood. Because of the worms." He chuckled. "Oh, yeah. I guess they don't have worms in Vancouver."

The windows were down, and gusts of dry hot air filled the van. I rubbed at my eye. Something tiny but scratchy had blown into it. "We have worms." I thought of Mom's compost pile.

"These aren't the kind in the ground, though. They're cankerworms," he said. "Famous Winnipeg worms. They live in the trees. They're at their worst right now. The babies have hatched, and now they're eating the leaves. You'll find out for yourself."

He waved his arm out the window, as if presenting me with something wonderful. All I saw were lots of tall older houses, crowded side by side in narrow yards. There were little kids everywhere. And trees, huge old trees lining the narrow boulevards. Looking straight ahead, I could see that the trees met over the top of the street, creating a canopy of green. But the leaves looked lacy.

"Yup. They do a lot of damage, chewing away. They're very destructive, the worms in the wood." He laughed. "Ergo, Wormwood."

"Air-go?"

"Ergo. It's Latin. For 'therefore.' There are worms in the wood. Therefore, I call all of this," he waved his arm, for the second time, out the window, "Wormwood." He laughed – a tight unnatural laugh, almost a heh-heh-heh like a cartoon character makes – and glanced over at me.

I looked out the window. "Mom told me you moved back to the place where you grew up. The Granola Belt. She said you'd fit right in with all the New Agers and old hippies that live around here."

"Denise called me that? New Ager? Heh-heh-heh," Dad went again.

I rolled up the window, and pressed my lips against it. "No. She called you an old hippie." *Welcome to Wormwood, Poppy*, I mouthed onto the dusty streaked glass. I watched the people on the streets. So far I hadn't seen even one tall red-haired woman.

🌳

At least I had my own room. I had this horrible image of sharing space with Dad's kid, who's, as Shakespeare would put it, in his mewling, puking stage.

"This is where we plan to eventually put the new baby. Calypso has been using it as her sewing room," Dad said, as he set the heavy gym bag, with a thump, onto the floor in the middle of the room. Calypso was standing in the doorway with the kid perched on her hip. His name was Sandeep. *Poor guy.* He was sucking his thumb. "But I moved her sewing machine and supplies into our bedroom, so you could use this. She sews, you know. Quilts. She's very talented."

A small murmur of protest came from Calypso's throat.

"Sure you are," Dad said. "She started a sewing group with a couple of gals, and they sell the quilts around the city to stores, and privately. Lots of people want 'em."

Gals. Only someone with a handlebar mustache, wearing pointy-toed cowboy boots, would say "gals."

I nodded, looking around. At least they hadn't gone wild with the paint in here, like they had outside. The other houses on the street were normal house colors – white with blue trim, gray with white trim, brown with darker brown trim. But not this one. The whole thing was painted a crazy deep raspberry. The trim was olive. When we'd stopped outside it and Dad said "Here's the old girl," all I could do was close my eyes.

They must have blown their decorating budget on the outside because everything inside – the walls and floors and furniture – was tired and secondhand-looking. No new paint anywhere. And this room was no different.

The wallpaper looked like it hadn't been changed since the house was built, which would have been a long time ago. It was faded stripes, with flowers in between the stripes. I couldn't recognize the color or the type of flower. Along one wall was a scratched dresser with an attached mirror, rippled and dotted with age spots, and an empty chest-high bookcase with glass doors. There was a single bed. A rocking chair sat in the middle of a circular rag rug on the discolored linoleum floor, and there was a yellowing lace curtain on the tall narrow window. The window was open, and the curtain hung limply in the still, hot air. I went to the window and looked down on the small and weedy fenced backyard, seeing a few trees, a huge truck tire – the inside filled with sand and toys – and a plastic wading pool, with only a shimmer of dirty water. I raised my eyes. Beyond, more trees and the roofs of houses. No mountains. No ocean.

One big bluebottle bounced on and off the bedroom screen with an exhausted, defeated buzz. The windowsill was littered with the assorted husks of dead insects. There was the smell of cat pee everywhere. I had to stop myself from pressing my forehead against the screen and weeping. I knew they were watching me. *What have I done?* I forced myself to think of my *M* Book, the reason I was here.

"Calypso worked most of the night to finish the new quilt for your bed," Dad said.

I turned around. The narrow bed, just a box spring and mattress – no headboard – sat in the far corner. The quilt was a colorful jumble of greens and blues, with yellow diamonds. It was the only bright spot in the room. *Who cares about a quilt? Couldn't she have cleaned up a little instead?*

"It's called Rocky Road," Calypso said. "The quilt pattern." Her voice was strangely small for such a tall woman. She was at least three inches taller than Dad. Sandeep was silent, watching me, his cheeks sucking in and out at his thumb. "And I've arranged the furniture in the proper alignment, so that the spiritual influences are right. Do you know about *feng shui?*" she asked.

I nodded, wearily. "It's big in Vancouver." The sinking feeling had almost hit my ankles by now. "So when are you having it?" I asked, raising my chin toward her huge bulk.

"Less than two months. Not long now," she said, dreamily, smiling a small secret smile. "You must be tired," she added. "Do you want anything to eat?"

I shook my head, bending to yank at the zipper on the gym bag. I couldn't believe how hard I had to work to keep my lips still. I wouldn't give them the satisfaction of seeing me cry. *Why do I feel like crying? This is where I wanted to be. This is where I was born, and where I can look for my real mother.*

"I ate on the plane. This goddamn thing," I said, giving the zipper one final tug.

"Gondam, gondamting," Sandeep said, finally taking his thumb out of his mouth.

Calypso cleared her throat and said "Poppy —" in a warning sort of way, but Dad interrupted her.

"Not now, Calypso. We'll let Poppy get settled before we read her the house rules."

Sure. House rules. We'll see how long it takes them to realize I don't do house rules.

FOUR

"Good Lord, Calypso," my father said, lifting his bare foot and giving it a shake. Drops flew from it.

"Yord!" Sandeep yelled from the table. He was kneeling on a chair, licking out his oatmeal bowl. He was wearing a yellow T-shirt announcing LOVE IS ALL YOU NEED. The T-shirt and nothing else. "Goodyord!"

Calypso turned from the stove where she was giving the big pot of oatmeal a stir, looked at my father's foot, then grabbed a rag, stained and unraveling, from the sink faucet. She lowered herself heavily to her knees, mopping up the puddle my father had stepped in. She gave my father's foot a swipe, too, but, I noticed, only after the rag was soaking. She didn't say anything, but her face didn't have the soft inner-peace look I'd seen last night. Instead, she looked tired, and the skin around her eyes was puffy.

"Can't you just put a diaper back on him?" Dad asked, holding the eyedropper over his glass of warm water. A slice of lemon lay limply on the bottom of the glass. He started letting the drops hit the water, counting under his breath.

"You know my feelings on that, Eric," Calypso said, holding the edge of the counter to pull herself up. She

30

looked at Sandeep, then at me. "The natural way, letting the child train himself, is best. Children instinctively know when the time is right. So we give Sandeep all the opportunities, and let him be the boss of his bodily functions."

Having to watch a two year old wave his bare bottom in my face at the breakfast table was enough to make me lose my appetite. I saw that there was a little potty-chair beside the fridge, and when I'd come into the kitchen this morning, I'd seen Sandeep sitting there looking at a book. But I don't think he was actually doing anything.

This morning, at 7:15, Calypso had come into my room. I felt like it was the middle of the night since, in Vancouver, it would be only 5:15. *Why couldn't she let me sleep?*

"Breakfast in ten minutes, Poppy," she'd said, as I tried to unstick my eyelids. "I want to talk to you for a minute, before you come downstairs. There are a few things that you should know, and we really didn't get a chance to say much last night."

I stayed where I was, my eyes still closed. "Mmm?"

"It's a delicate time for Sandeep. I'm trying to prepare him for the arrival of the new baby, as well as hoping that he'll train himself in the next two months so I won't have two babies in diapers."

Of course they would be cloth. I had already figured out that Calypso was too pure to stoop to anything that wasn't completely biodegradable.

"So. I need to make sure you never say the words 'go potty,' or anything to do with the whole toilet scene. It can cause a block in a child's development to force him to use the toilet when he's not ready." Then she left, whistling an unrecognizable melody. Her whistling was loud and powerful, mannish, somehow.

I nodded. *Right.* Calypso might know the theory, but so far − between last night and this morning − I'd seen Sandeep basically do whatever he wanted anywhere. And I'm talking number one *and* two. It's incredibly gross. Even Dad isn't sold on this one, although I'm starting to realize that he goes along with a lot of Calypso's weird ideas.

"Thirty-nine, forty." Dad put the dropper back into the bottle labeled ECHINACIA, and set it on the windowsill over the sink. There were lots of small dark bottles in a line. I had looked at them when I came down to the kitchen this morning. GINKO BILOBA, for memory retention, fatigue, and depression. SLIPPERY ELM, for digestive problems; DI GU PI, for lowering cholesterol. And the ECHINACIA, for prevention of colds and flu. I'd watched Dad taking a bunch of them this morning.

Now Dad drank until the glass was empty, then fished out the lemon wedge and sucked it.

"Why do you take all of those things, Dad?" I asked. "You're not sick, are you?"

Dad glanced at Calypso. "Nope. How does that saying go, Calypso?" he asked, but then, without waiting for an answer, pointed his finger at me and said, "'To take medicine only when you are sick is like digging a well only when you are thirsty – is it not already too late?' Some Chinese philosopher said that. Did you know that Calypso's mother was half Chinese?"

"No," I said, although there was definitely some interesting mix in Calypso's features. "So you don't even drink coffee anymore? I always remember you drinking gallons of it."

Dad shook his head. "No caffeine in any form," he said. "Hot water and lemon does the trick for me now. Calypso taught me about preventative measures."

"Your dad has come a long way in improving his physical and mental state since I met him," Calypso said. She was stirring the pot of oatmeal again. The stove was splattered with dried bits and pieces of food. Some of it looked like it had been there for months. "He says he'll never be a complete vegan, like me, but he does pretty well."

"You're a vegan? You don't eat meat?"

"Right," she answered. "I believe in a compassionate way of living. I don't exploit animals for any purpose. No meat, chicken, fish, eggs, or dairy products. We have mixed views on how Sandeep should be fed. Your dad insists he have cow's milk, although I've assured him that rice or soy milk will do."

Sandeep slid down from his chair and ran to put his arms around Dad's knees. He buried his face there.

"My Daddy," he said, lifting his face. "Not your dad. My Daddy."

Brat. "But I always have coffee in the morning," I said. "And sometimes a cappuccino after supper. We have a cappuccino-maker."

Dad just looked down and put his hand on Sandeep's curly hair. Sandeep was blond, like Dad. Calypso had very black hair in a thick braid that hung almost to her waist. She also had very black hair on her legs. She was wearing a grayish T-shirt that looked as if it had originally been white. It had a large pink stain shaped like the continent of Africa down the front. The cotton stretched grotesquely over her immense belly, and she was wearing green wrinkled shorts that were way too short for someone so pregnant, and with such embarrassingly hairy legs. Maybe she refused to shave them in empathy with all the exploited furry creatures.

"Don't drool on Daddy's pants, son," Dad said.

"You should say don't drool on *my* pants, Eric," Calypso said. "I keep telling you, you'll hold back his developing speech patterns by using that simplified language. You wouldn't talk like that to me. Or to Poppy." She looked over at me.

I was flipping through the newspaper, eating a piece of toast.

"Sandeep understands more than you realize," Calypso continued.

Sandeep pressed his mouth against Dad's off-white cotton pants again. I could see the beginnings of a spreading slimy patch, baby saliva mixed with oatmeal.

"Why don't you give him a few more months in a diaper? Obviously he's not interested in using the toilet." Dad gently disengaged Sandeep from his legs, picking him up. Sandeep settled against Dad's chest and put his thumb into his mouth.

Calypso put her finger to her lips and shook her head. "Please," she said, "no *T* word. See what that's made him do?"

I assumed she meant the thumb-sucking.

"No *T* word," Sandeep repeated, taking his thumb out of his mouth and looking at me, as if I'd said it. "No *T* word, Poopy."

I turned the page of the newspaper, concentrating on chewing my natural flax toast. It had all the flavor of wet cardboard.

"It's Poppy, Sandeep honey. Poppy, not Poopy," Calypso said, in a tired voice.

"Denise thought she looked like a Poppy," Dad said to Calypso. "As soon as she saw her, her little face all red, and her hair sticking up, just as red, she said, 'Look, she's like a little poppy.' I thought she looked like she'd stuck her finger in an electric socket."

"Thanks," I said.

"Just a joke," Dad said.

"Poopy," Sandeep said.

"He'll get used to your name, Poppy," Calypso said, "and to you. Just give him a little time." She came to the table and stood in front of me, her back to Dad and Sandeep. "He's used to being the only child," she whispered, "so he's a bit territorial about his father. He's already worried about his new brother or sister." She put her hands on her immense belly. "And then a half sister . . . well, it's a bit of an adjustment, you being here so suddenly and all. I'm sure you understand."

I didn't look up, showing great interest in an ad for small kitchen appliances. I wouldn't try to make her feel better by saying that I understood, or even by looking at her.

A bit of an adjustment for a two year old? My heart bleeds. What about me?

🌳

"So what are your plans for today?" Dad asked, as he was making his lunch to take to work.

"For starters, I'm going back to bed," I said. "Do you realize," I continued, glancing at my watch, "that at home the sun isn't even up yet?"

"We rise and shine early in this house," Dad said.

"You can shine as early as you like." I got up, yawning. "It's too early for me."

"I'd like you to give Calypso a hand with some of the work around here," Dad said, intent on grating a carrot over some lettuce in a plastic container. It was amazing that he could even find a clean spot on the counter to work. The place was covered with dirty dishes and empty containers and bags of rice and jars of pasta and at least three chipped and stained teapots of varying sizes. In other words, a disaster.

"So I'll count on you to help out. Maybe clean this place up a little, and watch Sandeep. Calypso's busy with her sewing these days, trying to get as much done as she can before the baby comes. She can't keep up with the demand for her quilts, and they bring in extra money."

I didn't answer. I was here on a mission, not to be a housekeeper or baby-sitter while Calypso worked. She had taken Sandeep upstairs to give him a bath.

"You still haven't told me what you're doing here," Dad said, grating hard and fast.

"Mom took off with her boyfriend. I didn't want to stay at Jan's." I wasn't ready to tell him the actual reason I had come to Winnipeg. It was hard to say "to find my real mother." It didn't feel like the right time.

"And there's no other reason? No trouble with your mom? With friends? Or a boyfriend?"

It's a little late to start acting like the concerned parent now, I felt like saying. I watched him rinse off the grater and put the lid on his salad. "Nope. I need some hangers. There are none in my closet."

He finally turned to look at me. "So what, exactly, do you intend to do with yourself?" he asked, ignoring my request.

"Do with myself?"

"Yeah. What are you going to do all day?"

"I'll find stuff to do. I'll probably listen to the CD's I brought," I said. "Watch some talk shows."

"Hmmm," Dad said. "We don't have cable. We mainly rent movies. We don't like Sandeep to watch television."

"No cable?"

"And no CD player. But there's a record player, and my record collection."

"Records?"

"All my blues records – B.B. King, John Lee Hooker, Etta James and Billy Holiday, Muddy Waters, Otis Rush, T-Bone Walker, and lots more. I've been collecting them for years. You're welcome to listen to them."

"No, thanks." I pulled an elastic out of my pocket and bunched my hair into a really short ponytail. Pieces of hair that weren't long enough fell back around my face. I blew at them.

"I guess I'll go out, then. I've got my bike, after all. That opens up a whole exciting world of possibilities." I couldn't stop myself from being mean to him. He looked so rabbity, standing there with the bag of carrots, blinking earnestly, looking genuinely puzzled.

"But first I'm going back to bed," I said. "And where are some clothes hangers? My stuff is getting wrinkled."

"I don't know. Ask Calypso. I want you to help her while I'm gone," he said. "I mean it, Poppy."

"Okay." I'd agree with him, whether I actually helped Calypso or not. I needed him on my side. I had a lot of questions.

Mom and I always had to scrimp, and didn't have a lot, but what we did have in our house was at least fairly clean. This raspberry house was a madhouse. Rivers of pee. No food fit for human consumption. No clothes hangers.

And cats. Cats everywhere. At least it seemed like everywhere, although when I actually counted, there were three. One yellow female, Etta. A gray striped one, Muddy, and a black one, with a white triangle under his chin. He was T-Bone. All three were grossly overweight, and had obviously been named by Dad.

"Nice kitty," Sandeep said, following Etta into my bedroom. I had just got back into bed after Dad left. I'd shut my door, but there was no lock on it. And it was obvious that a closed door meant nothing to a two year old. Sandeep was wearing an undershirt. His hair was damp and curly from his bath.

The cat jumped on my bed, and Sandeep followed.

"Go away, okay?" I said, quietly, to both of them. "I'm sleeping."

The cat started doing this digging thing on the quilt, scratching as if she were trying to uncover some lost treasure. Her paws flew, and Sandeep laughed.

"Stop it, Etta," I said, gently pushing at her. "Go away. Shoo."

"Shoo. Poo. Poo-poo potty head," Sandeep said, not laughing anymore, but staring at me. He brought his thumb up to his lips, then put it down. "Potty," he said.

"No. Poppy. I'm Poppy, not Potty." Then I wondered if he actually meant "potty." I threw back the covers, and the cat landed with a soft thump on the rag rug. Jumping up, I took Sandeep's hand, pulling him off the bed. "Do you have to go potty?"

He put his thumb in his mouth and started working on it.

I sighed, and led him out to the hall. "Go find your mommy now," I said. "And take kitty." I said it as nicely as I could manage, given the circumstances. The cat twined around his legs.

But he didn't go to find Calypso. Instead, he stood there, sucking his thumb and playing with Etta's tail, watching me. He started to make me nervous, just staring like that, so I went back into my room and took some clean clothes from the separate piles I'd made on the closet floor. I also grabbed my shampoo and conditioner and de-frizzer and mousse and brush and comb and hair dryer, and went into the bathroom. No lock on that door, either. Before I turned on the water, I looked for the lever to start the shower. There wasn't one. No lever and, when I looked up, no showerhead.

"Calypso," I called, opening the door. "Don't you have a shower?"

"No," she yelled from somewhere downstairs. "Just the tub."

I looked at myself in the small mirror over the sink. "You'd better get to work fast," I whispered to my reflection. "You don't want to stay in this dump any longer than necessary."

Halfway up and all around the tub was a gray, scummy ring. Beside a yellowing and chewed ferny kind of plant on the windowsill over the tub, there was a can of cleanser wearing a stiff rag like a top hat. Also on the windowsill, as still and seemingly lifeless as the plant and the cleanser, was Muddy, the fattest of the three cats. He stared at me, unblinking, Buddha-like.

"Get out," I said, but he didn't move. "Look, I'm not taking a bath with you staring at me." I pushed at his solid immobile mass, and he gave an indignant cat-squeak and then leapt, nimbly for such a hefty thing, onto the edge of the tub. "Keep going," I said, touching his back with the cleaning rag and opening the door. He winked at me with one topaz eye, then very haughtily swept out. I closed the door before he could change his mind.

I cleaned the tub and had a quick bath, washing my hair under the faucet, then got dressed.

There was nowhere to put all my hair stuff and, when I looked for an outlet to plug in my hair dryer, I couldn't find one. I stared at myself in the mirror again, running my fingers through my wet hair, then shrugged. *Who cares?*

Slipping down the stairs, nearly tripping over T-Bone, who was sleeping on the second step, I avoided the kitchen. I could hear Calypso whistling, the same loud tuneless whistle, punctuated by the off-and-on whir of a blender, and Sandeep banging something that sounded like a wooden spoon on a tin pot.

Outside, I took a deep breath of warm dry air. I had survived my first morning in the raspberry house.

🌳

I don't know what I was expecting. Did I think I'd get on the old clunker of a bike, ride down the street, and find my birth mother? That she'd recognize me, too, and that this emptiness, always hovering somewhere in front of my backbone ever since my mom and I stopped even attempting to get along, would suddenly fill up and I would feel okay again, like I was a whole, complete person? I guess, in a weird and very fantasy-like way, I did believe that something like that could happen. That's why I'd come to Winnipeg, wasn't it? To find my birth mother. I'd been born here, and my parents had lived here and adopted me at the Misericordia Hospital, somewhere in this area of the city.

I really had no idea where I was headed, only that I wanted to get away from the raspberry house before I ended up cleaning out a cat litter box, or that scary kitchen counter, or stepping into one of Sandeep's carefully deposited surprises. Maybe I could find an air-conditioned mall or some funky little shops.

Dad had told me about the worms, but I hadn't realized that Wormwood was at its height of wormdom. As I rode down the strangely deserted street on the wobbly bike left leaning against the side of the raspberry house, I discovered there were worse things than dirty counters to contend with in Winnipeg.

Webby things were everywhere, hanging and looping down from the trees. As I rode my bike along the street, they caught in my hair and on my clothes. It was the most horrible thing I'd ever experienced. The webs were sticky and thin, and some even swung across my face and into my mouth and nostrils.

"Yuck. Ugh," I said, wiping at my mouth. No wonder there was hardly anyone around. All of a sudden a long black skinny worm-thing swished across my line of vision, and I felt it attach itself to the top of my ear.

I swatted at it, shaking my head at the same time, and somehow steered my bike into a parked car. I wasn't going very fast, but still, I flew off the bike, skinning my knees and one of my palms on the gritty cement. The noise I made as I hit and then fell sounded, in my own head, like the head-on collision of two runaway trains.

"Hey! You okay?" someone called from somewhere.

I was too stunned and embarrassed to even look toward the voice. "Yeah, yeah, I'm fine," I said, picking up my bike, refusing to look at my stinging knees. "Fine," I repeated, then drove off, blinking away tears of pain and mortification.

I got to a busy main street, where there were no trees, and rode aimlessly for a while. I was hot and sweaty. The stores all looked commercial and uninteresting. My knees and hand burned. I wanted something greasy and filling, something with meat and cheese, to eat. And there was nowhere to go but the raspberry house.

Are you out there, Mom? I wasn't sure which mother I really meant. *Mom? Help.*

FIVE

The next morning it was Dad who wouldn't let me sleep in. "I can use your help today, Poppy," he said, standing in my doorway.

I opened one eye and glanced at my wrist. There didn't seem to be any clocks in this house, except for the grease-spattered one on the back of the stove, so I had to keep my watch on all the time. "7:15 again? It's 7:15 in the morning?" I couldn't get to sleep last night because of the time difference plus the two-hour nap I'd had in the middle of the afternoon, so had read in bed until after one in the morning. "I'm exhausted. Can't I just sleep?"

"No. I have a lot of deliveries today, and I just got a call that my partner is sick. There's one big carpet I can't carry by myself. You can help me."

"Me? Carry a carpet?"

Dad tucked his T-shirt into his jeans. "I'll see you downstairs. It's gonna be a hot one today. Wear something you'll be cool in." He glanced around the room, running one hand through his hair. "You've turned into quite the neat freak," he said.

"I'm not a neat freak," I said, sitting up and looking around. "I just put things away, that's all. It bugs me when I can't find anything because it's so messy." The books and CD's I'd brought were lined up on their own shelves in the bookshelf. My makeup was on one side of the dresser, my hair stuff on the other. All my pairs of shoes were side by side at the foot of the bed. My socks and underwear were in the dresser drawers, and for now, my clothes were in piles on the closet floor. One of tops – T-shirts and shirts and tank tops – one of shorts, one of jeans and pants, another of skirts. All waiting for hangers.

"Where'd you get that from, I wonder?" Dad said, his voice fading as he walked toward the stairs. "Denise was never all that concerned with being organized. And I sure –"

I got up and closed the door, shutting out what was left of his voice. 7:15. The smell of sandalwood filled my nostrils. Incense, this early in the morning. I sighed.

Sitting at the kitchen table with my head propped on my hand, I already felt a thin layer of sweat making my Divine Blue tank top stick to my back. I could see Calypso in the backyard with Sandeep, watering something along one side of the fence. "How come it's so hot already?"

46

"It's Winnipeg in late June. This isn't temperate Vancouver. Remember, Dorothy, you're not in Kan —"

"I know, I know," I said, interrupting. It wasn't funny the first time. "You guys don't have air-conditioning, or anything?"

Dad didn't answer. "Eat up. We have to get going."

I pushed my cereal away. It was unrecognizable dried fruit and grains that Calypso had mixed together and stored in a big jar on the counter. It didn't look too bad dry, but the soy milk turned it to a gooey mush. Even after I loaded it with brown sugar, all I could manage was a few spoonfuls. I'd give anything for a cup of coffee. I grabbed two bananas. "I'll eat these in the van."

"That's what you're wearing?" Dad asked.

I looked down at my favorite top and ironed shorts. My hair was pulled off my forehead with a band that matched my shirt. "Yeah. Why?"

"Pretty fancy for hauling carpets."

"It's not fancy. And all my stuff is like this. I buy it at the store where I work. Used to work."

He just raised his eyebrows, and I followed him out to the van, peeling one of the bananas.

The white van announced KARPET KING in big red letters on the sides and back. The seat was hot as I slid in, and the backs of my thighs stuck to the cracked vinyl.

"We'll stop at the warehouse and pick up the carpets first. There are two small ones, but like I said, there's a big one, and the apartment we're delivering it to is three floors up. No elevator. That's the only one I need help with. I can drive you home by lunchtime."

I glanced over at my father, at his long thinning hair already loosening from a pathetic ponytail, his handlebar mustache, and his the-eighties-called-they-want-their-glasses-back aviator glasses. As I leaned over to do up my seat belt, I saw a Tim Horton's styrofoam coffee cup stuck down the side of Dad's seat. In it was a crumpled square of wax paper, the kind they give out with a donut. *No caffeine of any kind. No sugar. Sure, Dad.*

I used the cup to stash my banana peels.

Dad wielded the van through the morning rush hour, constantly fiddling with the radio. He found a bluesy song, and said, "Listen to this one, Poppy. 'Dust My Broom.' This is a great tune." He turned the radio even louder, beating out the rhythm on the steering wheel. As he drove he'd yell out the window at other drivers every few minutes. No swearing, or even anything rude, just stupid stuff like "git along, little dogie," or "move that heap o' trash, Grandma."

After the carpets were loaded into the van, Dad drove to a part of the city with run-down houses and low brick apartment blocks. "This is it," he said, stopping in front of one of the blocks and checking his order sheet. Then he hopped out and opened the back doors of the van. "Come on, Poppy," he said.

I got out and stood beside him.

"I'll hop in and shove it out to you," he said. "Grab it and back up."

I did what he told me, almost buckling under the weight of the huge roll. "It's too heavy," I said, panting. "I won't be able to carry it."

"Sure you will. You'll see," he said, his sinewy arms bulging beneath the short sleeves of his T-shirt. "You go up the stairs first, so I'll have the weight. You don't have to go up backwards. Swing it onto your shoulder now."

I stood, my arms still around the deadweight. "You must be kidding."

"No. It's much easier that way. Come on. On three. One, two, atta girl – *three*."

I had to bend my knees to take the weight, and although it was easier to carry on my shoulder, with my arms up and around it, by the time we'd reached the second set of stairs my thighs were quivering. "I can't, Dad," I said.

"Almost there." His voice came from behind, muffled. "Just one more short flight. You're doing great."

We stopped outside a door, and Dad banged gently with his foot. "Mrs. Caspian?" he called. "Karpet King. We're here with your carpet."

The door opened almost immediately, and a very short, frail, white-haired woman stood back and let us pass. "You'll just have to leave it," she said. "Right here, in front of the door."

We lowered the carpet with a thud. "There you go," Dad said, wiping his forehead with his forearm. "Now all I need is a signature." He held out the order form and a pen.

Mrs. Caspian signed slowly, the pen shaking in her hand. "Thank you," she said, then looked at me. "Young girls today are so strong. My."

I shrugged.

Dad took the pen from her outstretched hand. "Okeydokey. We'll be on our way then."

"Well, thank you again," the old lady said.

As we stepped over the rolled-up carpet and started out the open door, Dad stopped, and I bumped into him. He looked back at the carpet. "Who's going to move your furniture, so you can put down the carpet?" he asked.

"Oh, I'll have to call in someone, perhaps the caretaker, or one of the young fellows in the building, and get them to help me whenever they have a minute."

Dad put the pen and folded order form in his back pocket. "We'll do it. Come on, Poppy."

I stood there for a second, not believing he expected me to help him move all the heavy old furniture, unroll the carpet, and then move the furniture back onto it. He had already started, hoisting a big chair and carrying it to edge of the room.

"Come on, Poppy," he said again.

I had no choice. It didn't take us that long, but by the time we finished my top and shorts were dusty. There were scuffs all over my sneakers. I put my hand up to wipe the sweat off my forehead, and I realized my headband was gone. It could be anywhere, under any of the furniture, or even under the carpet for that matter. I loved that headband.

"What a fine gentleman you are," Mrs. Caspian said to Dad, when we were finally leaving. "I can't thank both of you enough. Isn't he just the finest gentleman?" she said to me.

"Sure," I answered.

Back on Portage Avenue, Dad glanced over at me. "You hungry?"

I nodded. "Starving."

"I did bring my lunch from home," Dad said, nodding to his big cotton shopping bag full of plastic containers on the seat between us. "But I feel like something more filling." He put on his left signal, and turned into a McDonald's. "It's a good idea not to mention this to Calypso, though," he said, concentrating on studying the drive-through menu.

"You got it," I answered.

❧

I went on a few more deliveries, but like Dad had said, they were simple, not heavy, and then Dad drove me home. A few blocks from the raspberry house I took a deep breath.

"Dad? I was born around here, right?"

"Yeah. Over at the Misery. The Misericordia Hospital. We had to go there to pick you up."

"Did you see her when you got me?"

"Who?"

"The . . . my . . . the mother."

"See the mother?" Dad eased to a stop at a red light, and put one hand to his mustache. He twirled the end.

"Yes. My mother. My biological mother. Was she there when you picked me up?"

Dad kept twirling, then shook his head and stepped on the gas. "I don't remember that. I don't think so. No." He made a right turn. "No. Definitely not. There was an office, and we went into it and signed some papers, and they gave you to us." He nodded. "Yes, that's how it was." He made another right. "I think."

"You think?"

He nodded again. "Maybe. Or maybe . . . no, that was something else."

"Dad! Can't you remember anything? I mean, that was the day you *got* me."

Dad cut off a small silver Honda, and the Honda blasted its horn. "Sorry, buddy," Dad said, glancing in his rearview mirror. "That was sixteen years ago, Poppy." He tapped his temple. "The old brain cells have undergone a bit of damage in that time." He suddenly looked at me, his eyes owlish behind his glasses. "You don't do drugs, do you, Poppy?"

I blew out an exasperated *whoosh.* "Cut it out, Dad. So you never saw her, or talked to her? The . . . my mother?"

"I don't see why we would have. She gave you up."

"Do you know if she ever saw me? Held me, or fed me, or anything?"

We coasted up in front of the house. "Why all the questions?" Dad asked. "What's this all about?"

I looked at the house. Muddy and Etta were sleeping on the wooden railing that ran around the front porch.

"I thought . . . well, I wondered if I'd ever . . . you know, find her."

"The woman who gave you up?"

"Yeah."

Dad gave a snort. "That's about as likely as me winning the lottery."

"Do you buy tickets?"

"What?"

"Tickets. Do you buy lottery tickets?"

Dad's mouth twisted. "You think I've got money to spend on lottery tickets?"

"Well, then, for sure you'll never win. You've lost before you even start. You can't win if you don't take a gamble."

Dad revved the gas. "What are you talking about, Poppy? You've lost me. Listen, Calypso could probably use a hand with Sandeep about now. Why don't you go in and see?"

I got out of the van and slammed the door, then leaned in through the open window. "I've worked enough for one day," I said. "And you'd better wipe the ketchup off your mustache before Calypso sees you." Then I turned and walked, fast, away from the beat-up van and the raspberry house, walked up the wormy side-walk on my way to nowhere.

SIX

I passed kids playing on the sidewalks and people pushing baby strollers and old men with dogs on leashes. The midday sun was hot, and I had to keep dodging to avoid sudden encounters with swinging worms. When I was waiting to cross a street called Westminster, standing very still under the trees, I thought I heard the patter of soft raindrops. But the sun was shining, and the sidewalk wasn't getting wet. That's when I realized that what I was hearing was the rhythmic chewing of the cankerworms as they ate their way through the leaves. I noticed that a lot of the leaves were no more than tattered rags fluttering forlornly in the hot breeze.

After I'd crossed Westminster, I kept going until I hit the next cross street – Wolseley – then found myself on a street that suddenly curved. A street that looked as if once it had a certain glamour. Here the houses were bigger, set back from the road, some half hidden by massive old trees.

The street was empty except for a woman in a long green dress walking toward me. As I passed by her, I saw her stare at me and put her hand on her chest, but I kept going.

Seeing her put her hand to her chest made me realize my own was aching, partly from the heat, partly from tiredness, but also from something I didn't recognize that hurt more than being hot or tired. I slowed down. I wouldn't think about the expression on my father's face when he'd said "That's about as likely as me winning the lottery," when I'd confessed to him that I wanted to find my birth mother. He would be no help.

Don't think about it anymore today, I told myself. *Don't think about Dad, or about her. Whoever she is. Wherever she is.* I would go home and look through my *M* Book. That would make me feel better. The old, safe, hopeful thoughts.

I came to the end of the street. It was a dead end — nowhere to go but turn around. I headed back down the street, my feet feeling as if they were encased in cement. *The brave young heroine pushes forward. She is their only hope. She, and she alone, can save their lives.* The sun was creating a spotty dazzle through the ravaged leaves above. As I passed through a more open spot, the sudden brightness temporarily blinded me, and I squeezed my eyes shut, then opened them, and for a second was confused by the tall green bush right in front of me. But with my next step, when the glare was cut by the shadow of a house, I realized that what was directly ahead wasn't a bush at all, but a person. The woman in the long green dress, standing right in the middle of the sidewalk. As I came closer, I saw her begin to sway, and the ridiculous word "swoon" leapt into my head.

She seemed to grow shorter, right in front of me, and I realized that her knees were buckling, and she was going down. Sprinting toward her, I caught her by the shoulders. Her eyes were closed, and even though we were about the same height, she was so light that it was easy for me to hold her up.

"Are you all right?" I asked, panting.

Her eyes opened slowly, and she put one hand up to her forehead in that typically dazed "where am I?" thing that you see in movies, but don't believe anyone actually does. She was holding a square white purse in that hand. Around her neck was a thin gold chain, and hanging from the chain was a small gold key and an equally small gold leaf with finely etched veins. Her breathing was loud and coarse.

"I must sit," she gasped, and my head swiveled, looking for something for her to sit on, but of course there was nothing, and so I lowered her onto the grass beside the sidewalk. Her dress was made of something light and silky and, when she sat down, her legs folding gracefully under her, the dress billowed out around her like a cool cloud.

Now that I had stopped, I was suddenly aware of my hair sticking to my forehead, and the sweat stains growing under my arms and on the front of my tank top.

"Are you all right?" I asked again. I looked around, but the street was still deserted. "Should I go to a house and ask to use the phone, and call someone?"

She waved her hand in a *no* signal, then fumbled with her little purse. Opening it, she took out an inhaler and put it to her mouth, pushing down on it twice as she closed her eyes. She took a careful breath, then said, "Oh, no. I'll be perfectly fine in just a moment. Asthma. It's just my asthma, and combined with the heat, I got a little light-headed."

Her face was an awful color – almost like the oatmeal Calypso had cooked yesterday morning – except for a greeny-yellow on her temples and cheekbones.

"And I live right there," she said, limply waving her hand in a vague direction to our right. "I will rest for another moment."

I wasn't sure whether I should stay, but didn't know how to leave without seeming rude. I crouched beside her, listening to her breathing growing quieter.

The woman stared straight ahead for another long minute. "There," she said, putting the inhaler back in her purse and clicking it closed. She raised one hand to touch her hair. It was ash blonde, parted on one side and falling to just above her shoulders in soft loose waves. "I'm all right. Now, if I could beseech you to help me to my feet. . . ."

I put my arm around her back and sort of hoisted her. Along my arm and under my hand I could feel all her bones, her ribs along her sides, and the individual knobs of her vertebrae, as if her silky dress was just a delicate layer of skin, holding everything together.

"Thank you, my dear," she said. "How lucky for me that you came along when you did."

I realized, suddenly, that she was speaking with an accent. A southern accent. I hadn't noticed it before.

"Would you like me to help you to your house?" I asked.

"That would be lovely, but unnecessary," she said.

I kept my arm around her for that moment, afraid that if I took it away she would slither down into a boneless puddle, the silk dress shimmering and pooling around her.

"You're very strong," she said, turning to look directly at me. I could feel her breath on my face. There was a faint odor of something — like her dress — green and soft. Pleasant. I thought of Peter Rabbit, nibbling parsley in Mr. McGregor's vegetable patch to settle his stomach. Parsley suited this woman. She didn't look like she'd ever eaten anything tough and chewy, anything she'd had to tear and chomp. "I can feel how strong your arm is," she said now, still looking into my face. It gave me a creepy feeling, her so close, staring so directly into my eyes as if we were old friends.

I dropped my arm.

The woman swayed for a second, but then straightened her shoulders. "It's a great comfort — physical strength," she said. She snapped open her purse again. "I'm afraid it's something I've never had. Now, let me give you a little something," she went on. "For your help."

When I realized she was looking for money, I took a step away, shaking my head. "No. That's okay. It was no trouble."

She looked into my face. "Well, aren't you kind." She smiled, looking down into her open purse, and then gently closing it. "A kind stranger." She unexpectedly reached out and took my hand, shaking it gently and looking deep into my eyes again. "Ah have always depended on the kindness of strangers." Her southern accent was even more pronounced.

"Blanche DuBois," I said, giving the tiniest backward pull on my hand. But she held on to it. "*A Streetcar Named Desire.*"

Her dark blonde eyebrows, plucked so that they were a thin, arched line, rose into her smooth high forehead. The greeny-yellow I'd seen on her temples and cheekbones was gone, and now her cheeks had the faintest touch of pink. Her skin was very clear, with an almost translucent glow. She looked younger than I had thought at first, although I couldn't tell how old she was. She could have been anywhere in her thirties, and she was very pretty.

"So you've seen the play?" she asked.

"Yeah, I'm into acting," I said. "I've seen a lot of plays, or at least read them. Tennessee Williams is my favorite playwright." I glanced down at our hands. She still had a surprisingly firm grip on mine.

"I have played Blanche. More than once," she said.

I studied her face, but there was nothing familiar about it. "You're an actress?"

"Oh, yes," she said. She looked to her right. "Would you care to come along to my house, for a cool beverage?" The accent was gone, but she still had that look, too eager and friendly.

This was really creeping me out. "No, I better not," I said. I pulled my hand again, this time hard enough to let her know I wanted it back.

She looked down. "What lovely long fingers," she said, then put her palm against mine. "Look. Our hands are exactly the same size. Do you play the piano?"

"No," I said, jogging slightly, as if I was really in a hurry now, and had some place important to be.

"You have a pianist's hands. Like me," she said, pressing her palm harder.

I pulled my hand away and made a fist. "Okay. I have to get going now."

Her shoulders sagged. "If you must. Thank you again."

"No problem." I gave a sort of weak half-wave, and then turned and jogged up the street. As soon as I turned the corner, I stopped. Wormwood. What a place – full of worms and weirdos.

🌳

When I got back to the raspberry house, Calypso was sitting at the kitchen table with another woman. The table was covered with quilted squares as well as lots of strips of material.

"Oh, Poppy, I'm so glad you're home. Linnea, this is Eric's daughter, Poppy. Poppy, this is Linnea. She's another member of the sewing collective. And that's Tanner."

I looked at the little boy sitting on the chair beside Linnea. He was three or four, with short dark hair and huge brown eyes. He was wearing a baggy red and white polka-dotted bathing suit and a tight beige T-shirt with a stretched-out neck. He put his hands over his eyes when I smiled at him.

Sandeep, in his usual shirt-only attire, was busy pouring a glass of orange juice into his potty. "Potty head's home," he said, stirring the juice around with his hand and looking up at me.

"Linnea is one of the women who originally worked on your quilt," Calypso said. "When I told her you were coming, she suggested we give it to you instead of selling it."

I nodded.

"She spent hours and hours helping me get it done," Calypso added, her eyes sending me some kind of signal.

"Oh," I said, getting her message. "Thanks. It's . . . nice. It's a nice quilt. Thanks," I said again. The quilt was too heavy, especially in this hot weather.

"We could have chosen another one of our quilts for you, but I thought the Rocky Road pattern was sort of symbolic. Because that's how it can feel. Pretty rocky." Linnea had crossed her arms over her chest and was looking at me, her head tilted to one side.

"How what can feel?" I asked.

She uncrossed her arms. "Settling in to a new home," Linnea said, glancing at Calypso. Calypso was putting diamond-shaped pieces of fabric side by side, her lips thinned in concentration.

"But it's not my home," I said. "I'm just here temporarily. Really temporarily. Just for a while."

"Oh," Linnea said, then "oh," again, but quieter. She joined Calypso in fussing with the bits of material.

"We're laying out a new pattern," Calypso said, still looking at the material. Then she raised her head quickly. "Could you keep the boys busy for an hour? That's all it will take us to work out the details."

Linnea smiled brightly. "Calypso says you're great with kids. Tanner's pretty shy. He probably won't say anything to you, but don't worry about it. It takes him a while to warm up to people." Linnea had a wrinkled red bandanna tied over her long wavy dark hair, and wore navy corduroy overalls frayed along the bottom, a pink tank top, and flip-flops. There were dozens of braided bracelets around both her wrists, and a tiny tattoo of a feather on her right bicep.

"You could put Sandeep in his stroller and take them for a walk," Calypso said, still looking at the material. "Maybe stop at Vimy Ridge Park and let them have a few slides."

I didn't even answer. It wasn't like I had any choice.

"Sandeep should be all right in training pants," Calypso went on.

"I don't think I'll take that chance," I said, then held out my hand to Sandeep. "Come on, Sandeep," I said. "Let's go upstairs and put a diaper on you before we go."

"Diaper. Poopy-head," Sandeep said.

Tanner took his hands away from his eyes and giggled.

"Rescue the Perishing," Calypso said.

I stopped, Sandeep's hand in mine.

"It's the pattern we're doing," she said. "What do you think, Poppy?"

I looked at the older, finished pieces surrounded by brighter strips of material. "It looks . . . different," I said, for lack of a better word. The finished pieces looked really old, some of them worn around the edges.

"It's the kind of quilt you make by taking old blocks and making a new setting for them. I found some old torn quilts at a garage sale, and took out the usable bits," she said, touching the soft finished pieces. "For the Rescue the Perishing quilt, you take pieces from their original place and fit them into a new design. It takes some playing around, sort of like a puzzle. Sometimes all that's missing is one small detail." She picked up a block, turned it upside down, and set it back down. "And then, bingo! You turn the square a different way, and everything falls into place." She smiled at Linnea. "Look."

Linnea nodded, smiling back. She had a half-moon shaped scar by the outside corner of her right eye, but when she smiled, it disappeared.

Rescue the Perishing.

There were obviously more than a few of us around here that appeared to need rescuing.

It was close to supper time when I brought the kids home. I left them in the kitchen with Calypso and Linnea. Now there were piles of pinned squares on the table, and Calypso and Linnea were drinking peppermint tea. I went up to my room, and was just lying on my bed, thinking, when Calypso came to the door.

"Poppy, Linnea and Tanner have gone, but she wants to know if you'll baby-sit for her, tomorrow night. She's really stuck. She's a single mom. Would you? She could really use the help."

I shrugged, thinking of Linnea's raggedy overalls. *A single mom. More volunteer work, along with helping Calypso with Sandeep and helping Dad deliver carpets.*

"She asked what you charged, and I said I'd have to ask you. But she said it was okay, whatever it is, because she could tell that Tanner really liked you. So it's worth it to her."

Oh, great. Make me feel totally guilty. "Whatever she can afford," I said. Even if it was a pittance, anything was better than sitting around here trying to figure out what my next step would be. "Just tell me what time and where."

"It's not far. Palmerston Avenue. Straight down our street, across Westminster and Wolseley, and then left and a few streets over. They're big old houses, down by the river. Linnea rents the top floor of one of them. Do you think you can find it?"

I thought about the street where I'd seen the strange woman. "Yeah," I said. "I was walking around there this afternoon."

Calypso smiled. It was the first time she'd really smiled at me, not just those tight-lipped attempts I'd been getting since I got here. I realized, suddenly, that she was quite pretty.

"Linnea said Tanner really liked you. He doesn't like most people." She gave me a scrap of paper. "Here's the address. Seven o'clock tomorrow." She stepped into the hall, then stopped and raised her nose, sniffing. "Oh-oh. Sandeep!" she called. "Sandeep, where are you?"

I shoved the paper into my pocket. "Anywhere but on his potty, I'm sure," I said. I got a whiff, and pinched my nostrils with my fingers, breathing through my mouth.

I'm never going to have children.

SEVEN

When I rode my bike to Linnea's house on Palmerston the next evening, I discovered that I had been right; it was on the street where I'd met the fainting woman in green.

Linnea lived on the third floor of a neat old place that was once one home, but had been divided into what I could tell were three apartments – one on the main floor, one on the second floor, and Linnea's, on the very top. Hers was a big room with sloping ceilings. There was a strip of counter with a sink, a stove, and half-size fridge along one wall. Across the room was a large screen made of three quilts nailed onto a folding wooden frame. Through open doors I could seen a tiny bathroom in what looked as if it might have been a walk-in closet at one time, and a messy bedroom with an unmade double bed.

"I'll only be a few hours," Linnea told me. "Tanner will fall asleep soon." She smiled at the little boy lying on his stomach in the middle of the floor. He had on pajamas covered with purple and blue dinosaurs, and was walking a big plastic stegosaurus over some old pillows, making low growly sounds.

"My brother usually baby-sits, but he had to stay late

at work to do inventory tonight. He lives with us. Bye, lovey," she said, hugging Tanner. "Poppy will stay with you until Mommy comes home, okay?"

"We'll have fun, Tanner," I said, trying to sound enthusiastic. "Do you have any more dinosaurs?"

He nodded solemnly, pointing to a cardboard box beside the couch. I could see a jumble of plastic horns and tails.

"He likes to be read this, before he falls asleep," Linnea said, handing me a worn copy of *The Runaway Bunny* by Margaret Wise Brown.

"I used to like this, too," I said. I looked around the small space.

"Take anything you want to eat. The television is over there, and there are lots of books, and my brother has a CD player behind the screen. Just keep the volume down," Linnea said. "The old guy who owns this place – Mr. Hartley – lives in the ground-floor apartment. He's pretty strict with rules, but the rent he charges is worth it. I'd never find another place this cheap, so I try to stay on his good side."

Tanner looked worried when she first left, but as soon as I started to dig through his box of dinosaurs, he was very sweet and agreeable – one hundred percent better than Sandeep, I couldn't help but notice. When I saw him starting to yawn, I made him go to the bathroom and brush his teeth, and then I settled him in bed and read *The Runaway Bunny* to him.

It was such a sappy book, basically about a little bunny who says he's going to run away from his mother. But no matter where the bunny says he's going to run and hide, the mother bunny says she'll run after him because he's her little bunny. When the bunny says he'll become a fish in a trout stream and swim away, his mother says she'll become a fisherman and fish for him. When he says he'll become a rock on the mountain, his mother says she'll be a mountain climber, and climb to where he is.

I read each page slowly, pointing at the bunny hiding.

I remembered my own mother reading this to me, and when I got to the page where the bunny says he'll become a bird and fly away, and the mother bunny says she'll be a tree for him to come home to, I felt my eyes go all burny, and I had to stop for a second. *What is wrong with me?*

"Read, Poppy," Tanner said. "Read."

I cleared my throat and finished the book.

"Again," Tanner said.

So I read it a second time, and then again, and by the time I got to the last page for the third time, Tanner was asleep. I covered him, and then I sat on the edge of the bed with the book in my hand, running my fingers over the images of the mother and her little runaway bunny.

I tried not to think about my own mothers – the first Runaway Mother, who gave me up when I was born, and the second Runaway Mother, who ran all the way to

Greece to get away from me. The mother bunny was how mothers are supposed to be. They're not supposed to run away; they're supposed to run after their kids, loving them and looking after them, no matter how jerky the kid acts or what stupid things she says and does.

I put the book down and tiptoed out, then just walked around the apartment, exploring, which, I told myself, is not the same as snooping. I checked out the fridge. Hallelujah – regular people stuff. I made myself a bologna and cheese sandwich and took a can of Coke, then went and looked through a high painted-shut window that faced the street. There was no one around but an old man in the front yard, his arms resting on the gate. I wondered if it was Mr. Hartley. All I could see was the round bald spot on the top of his head, fringed with white hair.

Behind the screen there was a single bed with a sleeping bag on it, obviously where Linnea's brother slept. Beside the bed was a bookshelf made of bricks and planks of wood. It was full of books, some old hardcovered, the rest paperback. I read a few of the names – *Mythology: The Voyage of the Hero*, *The Library of Greek Mythology*, *A Dictionary of World Mythology* – not exactly light reading. There was an open bag of chips at the end of the bed. I took a handful – salt and vinegar, my favorite – and stared at myself in the round mirror on the wall over the bed as I ate the chips. Then I wiped my hands on my shorts and ran my fingers through my hair, so it stuck out around my face in the sort of funky look I liked. I stopped, looking at my hands, holding them up. The fainting woman who said she was an actress had said our hands were similar. I did a bunch of stuff with my hands, admiring the length of my fingers. "Ah have always depended on the kindness of strangers," I said, imitating the fainting woman's accent.

My voice was too loud in the quiet apartment. I quickly glanced around the screen, making sure Linnea or her brother hadn't come home unexpectedly and found me acting like a fool in front of the mirror.

Crunching a few more chips, I watched TV for a while, but was restless and jumpy and couldn't concentrate on the sitcoms. Finally I switched off the TV and just sat looking out the window that faced the river. The window was open, and I could smell a sweet odor, something in bloom. When the light had almost completely faded, I lit a candle that was in a holder on the wide windowsill. A cricket was chirping, or rubbing its legs together, or whatever it is that crickets do. Just one, all by itself, sawing away. It suddenly seemed like such a lonely sound. After a while, stiff from sitting in one position, I stood, looking out into the yard. In the dark, everything looked soft, in shades of gray and black.

I knew the river ran behind the house, and I tried to smell it, smell the water, but the sweet blossoming scent was too strong. I just stood there, breathing and listening, staring into the empty backyard. *Where are you, first Runaway Mother?*

Then something moved in the yard next door. Actually it wasn't in the yard, but in a tree, the one that hung over into this yard. There wasn't a fence between the properties, but lots of thick bushes.

I blew out the candle, trying to get a better look at what was in the tree. I could tell that it was something really big, moving around on one of the thick lower branches. It was too big to be an animal. As I watched, the thing slid down, landing soundlessly on the ground. I leaned my forehead and nose against the screen.

I couldn't tell if it was a man or a woman, but it was human. It started moving toward the house in a kind of creeping way; hardly more than a shadow, so thin and slow-moving – no, not slow, but careful – as if its body were glass. I leaned harder against the screen, trying to get a better look.

There was a click behind me, and I jumped, whirling around.

"Sorry. Did I scare you?" It was Linnea, closing the door. She flipped on a light switch. "Didn't you want the lights on?"

"No, you didn't scare me," I said, although I realized my heart was racing.

She went straight to the bedroom to check on Tanner, and I saw her bend down to brush his hair off his forehead, letting her hand rest there. "Was he okay?" she asked as she came out.

"Yeah. He was great. He went to sleep with no problem."

Linnea looked relieved. She pulled some bills out of her pocket and held them toward me. "Is this enough?"

I looked at the money. I saw that her fingernails were bitten, the skin around them red and sore-looking. "Hey, it's okay. I wasn't doing anything, anyway."

"No, no," Linnea insisted, pushing the money into my hand. "Take it."

I shoved it into my pocket. "Okay. Thanks."

"Maybe you can do it again sometime. If my brother can't."

I nodded.

"You'll be all right, riding home in the dark?"

"Sure. Who lives next door?"

Linnea smiled. "Becca Jell. Why?"

I told her about seeing the person sliding out of the tree.

"That's Becca, all right," Linnea said. "She's really a character. She was an actress once."

"An actress? I think I met her then, yesterday, here on Palmerston. Not really met, but sort of . . . ran into her."

"Yeah. Everyone on the street knows about her, even though she pretty much keeps to herself."

"What did she act in?" I walked to the door, and Linnea followed me.

"It was really only one Hollywood movie, in the eighties. *The Sorrow Club*. Hold on." Linnea went back to the television and ran her finger down the stack of videos piled on the floor, pulling one out. "Here it is. You can borrow it if you want." She handed it to me, and I shoved it into my backpack. "After this movie she did some commercials, but she doesn't like to talk about those. One was for a toilet bowl cleaning product, and I think another for a dishwasher."

"She told me she acted onstage," I said.

Linnea yawned, covering her mouth with her fist. "She could have. I don't know about that. Thanks again, Poppy."

Going down the dim stairway, lit only by a few wall sconces with those little night-light bulbs, I saw lots of old photos in frames lining the walls. I hadn't noticed them on the way up. Near the second floor I stopped, looking more closely at one of the pictures, and heard footsteps coming up the stairs.

It was a guy, holding a bike helmet. He had helmet head, his dark hair all sweaty and plastered to his skull. He was wearing some kind of uniform – beige shorts, with a wide plaid belt, and a matching short-sleeved shirt. A bad take on a safari outfit.

"Hi," he said. His teeth gleamed in the semi-light.

I pushed past him. "Hi," I mumbled back. With that hair and the sucky clothes, he was definitely not my type.

I had trouble opening the combination lock on my bike, and while I was working on it, I glanced at the house next door. There was only one small light glowing from a second-floor window. I was certain a shadow passed in front of the window, stopped, and then moved back. Almost as if someone was watching me.

I got on my bike and pedaled down Palmerston and, as soon as I got to the end of the street, I turned and saw the light go out, leaving Becca Jell's house in darkness.

EIGHT

The next morning voices from the kitchen woke me. I looked at my watch. 8:30. At least the pathetic 7:15 pattern had been broken. It must be because Dad and Calypso hadn't been able to get to sleep at their usual old folks ten o'clock bedtime.

I had ridden to the raspberry house from Linnea's to find every light on, and Sandeep screaming in Dad's arms.

"What's wrong?" I'd yelled, over Sandeep's high-pitched, hysterical wailing.

"We can't find Didi," Dad had said, turning over a couch cushion.

"Didi?"

"You know, Sandee's quilt. The little blue one with the hearts on it. He can't go to sleep without it. We've been trying to put him down since nine. But he's just getting more and more worked up."

"Didi! Didi! MY DIDI!" Sandeep howled, slapping at Dad's shoulder.

I glanced at my watch. Close to eleven. Calypso'd waddled in from the kitchen, breathing hard. Her face was pale, almost waxy. "It's not in the backyard."

"Take him," Dad had said, handing Sandeep to her. The kid's face was smeared with tears and gunk from his nose. Dad pulled the couch out from the wall and crammed his head down to look for it.

"We've searched everywhere we can think of," Calypso said, rubbing Sandeep's back. "It's not there, Eric?" she'd asked, as Dad pulled his head out. There was a cobweb caught in one of his eyebrows. He pushed the couch back with an angry shove.

"I'm going to bed," I yelled. Nobody seemed to hear me.

I went upstairs and closed my door, but the thin layer of wood did nothing to deaden the brat's frenzied shrieks. I spent a few minutes posing in front of the mirror, trying out different expressions – shock, horror, pain. It wasn't hard, listening to Sandeep.

I got out a pair of boxers and a T-shirt to sleep in, then opened my closet door to put my clothes into the cardboard box I was using for a laundry basket. As I tossed them in, something caught my eye. Something that wasn't my own dirty clothes.

"I've got it!" I called, waving the faded and frayed baby quilt over my head as I ran down the stairs and into the living room. "I found Didi!"

There was an instant of dead silence as Sandeep's last long scream ended in the middle of a crescendo.

"It was in my laundry box," I'd said. "He must have been playing in my closet."

Dad and Calypso sighed in unison – a long, exhausted exhalation of air. Sandeep hiccuped, holding out his arms. "Di." The word hung, caught in the middle by a sob. "Di," he finished.

I'd put it into his arms, and he buried his face in it. "My Didi," he whispered, then looked up at me. "Poppy found Didi."

"You better say thank you to your sister," Dad said.

An odd feeling washed over me. *Sister*. I'd never been called that before. I'd never thought of myself as a sister, even when I heard about Sandeep being born. "It's okay," I said. "He doesn't have to."

"Sank you, sister," Sandeep said, putting his face into the quilt.

Calypso put her hand on my shoulder. "You are a lifesaver," she'd said, her tired face attempting a smile. "Now. Let's all try and get some sleep."

🌳

I lay in bed for a few more minutes, wondering about a lot of things. Like what caused the inexplicable shiver I'd had when Sandeep called me sister; why Becca Jell was sitting in a tree in the dark; why the guy I'd passed on Linnea's stairway was wearing a cheap imitation of a safari suit; what my mother was doing in Greece right now. I also wondered about my real mother, maybe who was somewhere right here in Winnipeg. I could have passed her on the street, for all I knew. Stranger things have happened. People do buy one lottery ticket and win six million dollars.

There was an unfamiliar smell wafting in through my open bedroom door. Unfamiliar because it was actually good. I chose a clean pair of shorts and another of my favorite Divine Blue tops – this time a T-shirt with tiny yellow ducks all over it – and padded down the stairs in my bare feet.

"Do I smell pancakes?" I asked, coming into the kitchen. Dad was standing in front of a griddle with a lifter in his hand.

Sandeep was on Calypso's lap, and she was putting a bib around his chubby little neck.

"Made with rice flour," Calypso answered. She put Sandeep into his high chair, then rested her elbow on the table and put her cheek against her hand, yawning. "You're going to be really late for work, Eric."

"I'll work a couple of extra hours this evening. They always want people to do late deliveries on Friday."

Friday. I'd actually lost track of the days. At home, Friday had a huge sense of anticipation – the weekend beginning. *What difference do weekends make here? Every day is the same.*

"Dad," I said, "how far is the Misericordia Hospital from here?"

Dad brought over a platter of pancakes. "Not far. A few minutes by car."

"That's where I was born," I said to Calypso.

"Poor thing," she answered.

"Because my mother gave me up?" I asked.

Calypso frowned. "Well, that, too. But I was imagining how terrible the birth process must have been for you in a hospital. Being pushed out into a sterile, cold room with glaring lights that would have hurt your new eyes. Being caught by gloved, impersonal hands. Or maybe even pulled out with forceps. Do you know if they had to use forceps on her, Eric?"

Dad shrugged. "How would I know?"

"Did she have bruises on her temples when you got her?"

"I don't remember."

"It's awful – the whole hospital scene," Calypso said. She forked a pancake onto Sandeep's plate. "That's why I'm so glad Sandeep wasn't scarred by the birth experience."

"What do you mean?" I asked, taking two pancakes.

"Well, I had him at home, of course. With Eric and a midwife to assist. It was a beautiful experience. Wasn't it, my darling?" she asked, putting her hands on Sandeep's cheeks and staring into his eyes. "You remember swimming toward the light, don't you? We had only candles in the room," she said, glancing at me, "to ease him into the world. And he gently swam toward the light. That's what his name means, in Hindi. Light. And he is my light, the light of my life," she said.

81

I looked at Dad. He had spread jam on his pancake and was now chewing, thoughtfully.

"You helped deliver Sandeep?" I asked.

He nodded.

"And it will be the same with baby Pan," Calypso said, putting her hand on her abdomen. "I hope you'll help, too."

"Baby Pancake!" Sandeep said, picking up a piece of pancake in his fingers and squishing it. Then he shoved it into his mouth.

"Pan?"

"Yes," Calypso said dreamily. "His or her name will be Pan. Pan was the god – or it could have been goddess, why not? – of all the creatures of the forests and meadows. And when this baby was conceived, in late November, it was a bitterly cold night. But Eric had brought home a huge bouquet of flowers, just to cheer me up. It had been a hard month; Sandeep had an ear infection and wasn't sleeping well." She ran her index finger along the shell of Sandeep's ear. He laughed. "So we put the flowers by our bed, and they smelled so sweet, and when I closed my eyes I imagined it was a beautiful summer day, and I was in a huge meadow, surrounded by wildflowers, and then Eric –"

"Is there any honey?" I asked. I really didn't want to hear this. I couldn't ignore the fact that Calypso was pregnant, but I didn't have to hear the details of her and my father. *Can't she see that I'm completely mortified by her talking about their sex life?*

"No. No honey. Bees' homes are destroyed in the process of extracting honey from their hives," Calypso said. "The jam is very nice. Plum. It's organic."

I reached for the jar. "Thanks for the offer. Of helping with . . . Pan," I said, telling an outright lie. *Yeah. As if I would be part of that whole messy business.* "But I won't be here, anyway. I shouldn't be here that long. So Dad, do you remember anything else?"

Dad wiped the last piece of pancake around in the jam on his plate. "About what?"

"What I was asking you about yesterday?" I glanced at Calypso. "I'm trying to find out if Dad can remember anything about the day he and Mom got me."

Dad finished chewing. "I can't say I remember any specific details, although I do remember that it was a bit of a shock, you know, getting that phone call."

"What do you mean, getting that phone call? About me? Why was it a shock?"

Dad pushed his chair away from the table and stood up. "We'd had our name in for seven years. We'd basically given up. And your mother and I were already . . . well, things weren't going that well between us."

"But you took me anyway."

"Your mother wanted a baby. And we thought we could work out the problems between us. We'd made a lot of changes in our lives – both of us working hard, really settling down. We thought that a baby would help."

"My mother wanted a baby, you just said. Are you saying *you* didn't want me?"

Dad settled his cap on his head. It was peaked, with WINNIPEG FOLK FESTIVAL written across the front. "I didn't say that at all." He bent down beside Sandeep's high chair and kissed him on the cheek. "Why are you asking me all of this, anyway? Why didn't you ask your mother?"

I watched him kiss Sandeep again, then make bubbly growling sounds into the fat baby cheek. Sandeep laughed – a delighted, high laugh. I don't remember my dad ever kissing me.

Mom never tells me anything, I thought, but didn't bother to say it to Dad. He didn't really want to know.

After Dad left I put *The Sorrow Club* into the VCR. I had to push all three cats off the couch, and tried to wipe off the layer of cat hair before I sat down.

Becca Jell had a secondary role in the movie. She wasn't bad. She looked much the same as the woman I had seen a few days ago, except younger, and her hair was platinum blonde. Just before the movie ended, Calypso called me.

"Yeah?"

"Please, Poppy, take Sandeep out for a while."

"Calypso. I'm trying to watch a movie. Can't he play around here?"

Calypso came into the living room, carrying Sandeep on one arm and Didi draped over the other.

"I really need to meditate. After last night I can feel that my *chi* is totally out of alignment."

Sandeep put his index finger up his nostril.

"Your what? Sandeep," I said, frowning, "take your finger out of your nose. That's not nice."

"*Chi*. The vital life force that resides in our breath and body. Mine is all haywire. And I need to meditate to feel right. Can't you just put him in his stroller and go for a brisk walk? He'll probably fall asleep. He's already tired."

"But Calypso . . ."

"Please, Poppy? This is important. My midwife is coming over, and I want to be in a good space for our meeting. I want her to pick up on my positive energy."

Sandeep put his other index finger into his other nostril. "Walk," he said. "Poppy take Sandee for a walk." His voice was plugged and hollow because of the fingers in his nose.

"Your name is Sandeep, darling," Calypso said. "Not Sandee. Sandeep. My light." She handed him Didi.

"Myligh," Sandeep repeated, taking his fingers out and rubbing the edge of the quilt along his cheek. "Poppy take Myligh walk. Myligh Sandee walk."

Sighing, I switched off the movie and held out my arms. As Calypso passed him to me, she whispered, "Do you notice that he's not hearing final consonants? He's always calling himself Sandee. No *P*. And now no *T* on light. I should have his hearing checked." The lines on her forehead were showing more than usual.

I breathed in the smell of Sandeep's warm little neck. I had noticed that Dad only called Sandeep Sandee when Calypso wasn't around. "I don't think you have anything to worry about," I said. "I'm sure his hearing is just fine."

"Walk," Sandeep shrieked. "Now! Now! Now!"

"He hears just fine," I shouted, to make myself heard, but Calypso was already heading back toward the kitchen.

"Do you want to go potty before we leave, Sandeep?" I asked him.

"No!" he shouted, shaking his head so that his curls bounced around. "No potty." He put his thumb in his mouth.

I sighed, carrying him upstairs to his room, where I put a double cloth diaper on him, pinning them together firmly, then slid on a pair of rubber pants. I could hardly work his shorts on over the bulk.

My kingdom for a disposable diaper.

NINE

I pushed Sandeep's stroller to Vimy Ridge Park, found a swing without a broken chain, and swung him for about ten minutes. Then I put him back in his stroller and I walked up and down about fifteen streets, avoiding the most wormy ones, but Sandeep didn't show any signs of falling asleep.

I didn't mean to, but after a while I found myself on Palmerston Avenue again. I walked slowly past Linnea's place, and even slower past the house next door. There was something about it that drew me to it.

At the end of the street I turned around and walked back. When I got to the house next to Linnea's again, I stopped and studied it.

It was a large redbrick two-story, with a veranda running across the front. The gleaming white paint on the front door and window trim looked fresh. There was a high black wrought-iron fence along the front of the yard. Like the house, the yard was very well kept and beautiful. The grass was cut, and there were rosebushes in a circular flower bed in the center of the lawn. There were a lot of big old terra-cotta pots filled with geraniums and a trailing ivy lining the walkway leading to the house.

I knelt down in front of Sandeep. "Should we see if Tanner is home?" I asked him. "Do you want to play with Tanner?" I thought that maybe this morning I could ask Linnea more about Becca.

Carrying Sandeep, I went into the front hall of Linnea's place. But before I even put my foot on the first stair, one of the doors on the main floor opened, and an elderly man stepped out.

"May I help you?" he asked. "You're not trying to sell anything, are you?"

"No. I was going upstairs," I said.

He studied my face, then Sandeep's.

"I baby-sat Tanner for Linnea, last night," I explained. It seemed as if he might not believe me. "And I wondered if Tanner wanted to play with Sandeep. My . . . brother," I said.

"My brudder," Sandeep echoed.

The man's face relaxed. He looked at his watch. "She would be at her job at the food bank this morning," he said. "She takes the child with her. If she comes directly home, she should be here in the next half hour. You're welcome to wait in the backyard."

The man was very neatly dressed, in gray suit pants with a sharp crease up each leg, a crisp white shirt, and black suspenders. The only thing that didn't suit his outfit were worn black-leather slippers on narrow, almost dainty, feet. He had a small, bristly, white mustache, but his cheeks were clean shaven. What was left of his thin white hair was combed straight back, not quite covering the round bald patch. I could see the lines the comb left in his hair.

"I'm the owner of the house, Mr. Hartley. It's quite all right to wait in the backyard."

Sandeep was squirming in my arms. "Well, okay," I said. "We'll wait for a bit."

"If she arrives, I'll let her know you're here," he said.

Thanking him, I put Sandeep back in his stroller and pushed it around the house on the uneven paving stones that formed a walk. The backyard was overgrown and unkempt, the grass sprinkled with dandelions. The river sparkled just beyond the wild growth of willows at the end of the property.

I took Sandeep out of his stroller and held his hand as we walked around and around the yard. The long grass was soft, brushing against my ankles, still damp with morning dew where the big old trees that divided the yards cast shadows. There was a sagging back step, with a couple of bikes chained to the rails. We sat on the step for a few minutes. I found a trail of ants to show Sandeep. Each ant was carrying a crumb, or a grain of something, and we watched them. I had to hold Sandeep's hands after he tried to pick one up and flattened it. "Aw gone," he said, sadly, looking at the black smear between his fingers, but then he went for another one.

As I led him away from the ants, I found half of a delicate robin's egg in the grass, and picked it up, showing it to Sandeep.

"It's the same color as your T-shirt," I said to him. "Turquoise blue. It's an egg from a baby bird."

Sandeep leaned toward it, sniffing the edge of the shell. "Mommy's baby egg," he said, putting out one finger to touch the shell sitting on my palm.

"Not your mommy's baby. A bird's baby. A baby robin."

"Baby Pan," he insisted, his voice edged with crankiness. "Baby egg." He rubbed his eyes.

"Come on, Sandeep. Let's go sit under that tree." I spread Didi in the shade of the huge old tree that grew in the yard next door. Its branches hung low, into this yard.

Sandeep took one edge of Didi and rubbed it on his cheek. I lay on my back in the grass beside Sandeep, and looked up at the tree, and then at the house, and realized that this was the tree that I'd seen Becca Jell in last night. The branch that hung over us looked dead. All of the leaves – not just the tattered worm-chewed ones, but also the whole smaller ones – were brown and brittle.

Sandeep scrambled to his knees, holding out his chubby little arm. "Rown and rown," he said.

"I don't know what that is," I said. "What's rown and rown?"

"Rown and rown garden," he said. "Teddy bear. Do yike Daddy."

I ran my finger along his arm. The skin was so soft. "I don't know what game Dad plays with you." *He never played any with me.* I tickled Sandeep's arm.

He laughed, high and screechy. "Again, again," he said.

I tickled it again. He laughed again, then looked at me, grinning.

"Poppy," he said. "Poppy tickle."

I smiled back at him. He had adorable little baby teeth. Actually, he was a sweet kid, when he wasn't acting like a brat in front of Dad and Calypso. *Why do I feel so mad at him all the time?* "That's all now," I said. "No more tickling."

He pointed to the river. "Water," he said.

"Yes. That's the river. Now lie down again."

He actually listened to me, and I settled myself on my side, facing him. "Soon Tanner will be here," I said. I touched his cheek. He had incredibly long eyelashes, dark, in contrast to his blond hair; definitely Calypso's eyes. "Go to sleep for a few minutes, baby."

"Not baby," he protested, but quietly. He turned on his other side. "Sandee not baby," I heard him whisper to himself. "Sandee big boy. Pan robin baby."

I smiled. Maybe he could convince Calypso to call the new baby Robyn. The sun filtered through the rustling leaves, warm on my face. I closed my eyes, hearing Sandeep still whispering to himself.

I thought, again, about how I'd seen Becca Jell in the tree last night. About her in *The Sorrow Club*. The sun felt so good.

"Sleep now, Sandeep," I murmured, my eyes still closed.

The piano music was beautiful, soft and gentle, something classical, almost like a lullaby. I knew I was still half asleep, but felt I could stay like this forever, listening to the soothing music, the grass soft under me, my cheek cradled in my hand. I held my other arm up, looking at my watch. We'd been sleeping for at least half an hour. Linnea must not have come home.

The music stopped and, as my ears adjusted to the quiet, I heard another sound. Crying. But not Sandeep's, not childish crying. This was the grown-up kind – deep, quiet sobs. *Where is it coming from?* I sat up and turned to look at Sandeep.

Didi was there, in a rumpled heap. But no Sandeep.

My head swiveled around the yard. "Sandeep?" I called, jumping to my feet. "Sandeep!"

At that moment the music started again, but not the calming, airy music I'd first heard. This time it was pounding, hard chords, fierce and angry.

"Sandeep!" I yelled, hurrying toward the walkway, thinking about the street, Palmerston Avenue; about speeding cars screeching out of control as Sandeep toddled off the curb; of huge unleashed dogs dripping foam around needle-sharp teeth while Sandeep reached out, saying "doggie." Of perverts on the lookout for unsupervised children. And then I stopped, as if a hand had grabbed me by the back of my shirt. *The river.*

I turned and raced toward it. *Please, please, not the river. Don't let him have gone to the river.*

I had to struggle through the thick willows that grew along the edge of the high bank. There was no gentle slope to the water, just a sudden six-foot drop into the quickly flowing brownish-green water.

I kept standing there, looking down at the water, then back to the house. "This isn't happening," I said, trying to hold down the panic filling my chest. *But it is.*

"Sandeep!" I screamed, furious at the crashing piano music that was covering the sound of my voice, and maybe the sound of Sandeep calling for me, or crying.

As I looked toward Linnea's house again, I realized that the piano music was coming from Becca Jell's, and at that very instant I saw a flash of turquoise through the bushes that ran between the yards. The music swelled, growing even louder. I rushed toward the turquoise, pushing through the thick hedge, scratching my arms and legs and suddenly breaking through into the back-yard of the house next door.

Sandeep was there, turning the corner of the house. All my images of what might have happened to him instantly faded. Now I was mad at him for not answering me.

"You come back here," I yelled, running after him, along the back of the house. There was a huge, floor to ceiling window that faced the river. I realized it was a sliding patio door, open, with a screen. As I ran past, I could see a piano, and at it was a shadowy shifting shape, swaying over the keys.

I raced around the corner of the house to see Sandeep further along the side, crawling up onto a low step, and reaching toward the handle of a screen door there.

"Sandeep!" I yelled, and in that instant luck was on my side. The music ebbed, for just a moment. "No," I yelled, as loudly as I could. "No, Sandeep. Don't go in there."

At my voice, the music stopped. Sandeep looked over his shoulder at me, smiled his sweetest baby smile, then pulled the door open and stepped inside. The door shut behind him with a solid click, and he was gone.

TEN

Okay. He hadn't drowned. He hadn't been hit by a car, attacked by a vicious animal, or carried off by a baby snatcher. He was safe.

All I had to do was march up to the door, open it, and call his name. Maybe step in, and take him by the hand and lead him out. I jumped onto the step and looked through the screen door. There was a landing, with a flight of stairs going to the basement and a few steps leading up to a kitchen, an old-fashioned kitchen with a high ceiling and equally high glass cabinets.

"Hello?" I called. There was no answer. "Sandeep!" I called, louder, pressing my face against the screen and looking toward the kitchen. "Sandeep, come here. Come to Poppy."

"What do you want? What are you doing here?" The voice was so unexpected, so harsh, that I jumped back, almost falling off the step. An old woman stood on the landing, staring through the screen at me. *Where had she come from?* It must have been the basement, although she would have had to be really fast – for such an old woman – to get up the stairs without me seeing her coming. She was wearing a navy blue dress, with shiny black buttons up the front.

"Who are you? What do you want here?" she asked again. She had an accent — not strong, just a slightly different rhythm to her words. She stepped closer, then raised her right hand.

She had an ancient golf club in it.

"No," I said, putting my own hand up. "No. I'm just looking for my . . . for a little boy, a baby really."

"There are no children here," she said, taking another step closer to the screen. In her funeral kind of dress, her thin gray hair chopped off so close to her head that I could almost see the dull gleam of her skull, she looked like one of those horrible old housekeepers from a black-and-white movie. The golf club swooped toward the screen.

Go for innocent. Big-eyed and trusting — the Bambi look. Just a little scared, too, just enough.

I stepped back. "No, you don't understand." I made my eyes even wider. "He's with me. I'm looking after him. I was next door, and I . . . and he ran over here." I wouldn't give this old bat the satisfaction of knowing I fell asleep. "I saw him come in the door. Please." *Softer, now.* "Please?"

"The door is locked," she said. "No one comes in here."

"No. It isn't locked," I said, putting my hand on the handle and pulling. The door opened. "See. See? It isn't locked." I let the door go, so it closed again. "And he came in here. He's only two years old. Can you find him? Please? His name is Sandeep."

There was a shuffling sound from the kitchen. Then a figure came into sight, a slight, girlish figure. She had on a long-sleeved white blouse with the sleeves rolled up, loose white pants, and white sneakers. And she was carrying Sandeep.

"Look, Rakel," she crooned. The name sounded like rack with an *L* on the end. "Look. An adorable little boy. I was playing the piano, and he just appeared. He came from nowhere."

The voice was familiar. It wasn't the panting one, gasping for air, or the one with the fake southern accent. This was the voice from *The Sorrow Club*.

"It is the girl's child," the old woman said. "This girl's." She waved the golf club in my direction.

Ignoring it, I stepped up to the screen. "Sandeep," I said, "why did you run away from me? I'm sorry," I said, looking at the woman in white – Becca Jell, the actress. "I was next door, and he just ran in. I couldn't stop him."

"Rakel," the woman said, turning toward the old woman, "where are your manners? Please, young lady, do come in."

"No," I said. "I should take him home now. Come here, Sandeep."

"Sandeep have juice," he said, one arm resting comfortably on Becca Jell's shoulder.

"Certainly. Certainly you may have some juice, my darling," she said. "Rakel, get a glass of juice for this lovely child. And you must come in," she said to me. "Come, come," and she walked away, with Sandeep looking over her shoulder at me.

I really had no choice. The old woman – Rakel – hadn't moved. I gently pulled the screen door open. "I guess I'll have to come in. To get him," I said, still eyeing the golf club.

She leaned it against the wall, shook her head, and made an angry smacking sound with her mouth. Then she stomped up the stairs into the kitchen. She was wearing black stockings and black shoes, even though it was a hot day. Her shoes were that old-lady kind, with round toes, laces, and solid sensible heels.

I stepped onto the landing, not sure whether to follow her or not. I saw her open the fridge – a really old style of fridge, white and humpy – and take out a carton of apple juice. Then she reached up and took a high delicate-looking glass tumbler from one of the cabinets over the sink.

"Oh, no," I said. "He'll knock that over. Do you have something smaller? Plastic?"

She turned to me. "We do not own plastic glasses."

"A cup, then? Like a coffee mug? He's not that good at holding stuff. He's only two," I said, suddenly feeling I had to defend Sandeep. "He usually drinks from a bottle. Or a baby cup with a lid."

Rakel opened the cupboard again. "This is what we have." Her voice was still as unfriendly as it had been when she was brandishing the golf club at me.

I moved closer and looked in the cupboard. Everything was so fancy – fragile china plates painted with tiny rosebuds, elegant white cups and saucers with gold trim. Glasses so thin that it looked as if you would break them just by holding them.

"You don't have anything . . . plainer?"

"It is our kitchenware. Our good china is in the dining room," Rakel said, with a definite snobby tone.

I looked around the long room. There, upside down in the drying rack on the counter next to the sink, was a small empty jam jar. "Give him that," I said.

"It is a jar."

"I know. But it's small enough that he can hold it."

Rakel grabbed the jar and poured it full of apple juice.

"Not so full," I said. *Doesn't this woman know anything about kids?*

She looked at me, pressing her lips together so hard that they were stitched into a thin even seam. She marched to the sink and slopped out half the juice.

"You sit," she said to me, pointing to the long wooden kitchen table surrounded by high-backed wooden chairs. "Sit, and wait."

"No," I said. She was a bit scary, but she wasn't going to make me sit in the kitchen. "I'll come with you. I want to make sure Sandeep is okay."

The seam that was her lips disappeared completely. She turned and went through a swinging door. I followed her, reaching out to stop the door from swinging into my face.

"Sandeep," I heard her mutter, as we passed through a huge dining room, with dark wood partway up the walls. There was red velvety wallpaper with a swirly design on it above the wood. The heels of her shoes made hard clacking sounds on the hardwood floor. "What kind of name?" She was still shaking her head.

I hurried behind her, glancing at the immense table surrounded by at least a dozen chairs. There was a strong clean lemony odor of polished wood, along with something else, in the darkened room. The one high wide window was completely draped with a heavy lace curtain. I realized what the other smell was. Emptiness. The room smelled and felt like it was never used.

Rakel let the next door swing toward me, too. She was making it completely obvious that she was ignoring me. The room I stepped into was the complete opposite of the dark unused-looking dining room. This one was flooded with light. I had the immediate impression of flowers and soft cushions and life. It was the room that faced the river, the one with the piano.

Becca Jell and Sandeep were sitting on the piano bench. She was holding Sandeep's fingers over the keys, pressing them down to make the first few notes of the soft lullaby I'd heard earlier. I looked at her fingers, then down at mine.

They both turned as Rakel walked toward them, holding the jar of juice. I saw the glint of gold in the open neck of the woman's shirt.

"Poppy," Sandeep said. "Poppy, Poppy."

"Yes," the woman said. "I thought I recognized you. You're the kind stranger who came to the aid of a damsel in distress."

"Hi, again," I said. *Should I let on that I know her name? In a flash I decided not to.* "Blanche DuBois, right?"

She smiled. Her teeth were small and even, like a child's. "Actually, I'm Becca Jell."

She said it the way she might have said "I'm the queen of England" – as if it were unnecessary, but she was just being polite to a lowly subject.

"Jelly belly," Sandeep said, putting one finger on a piano key and pressing three times. It was a high key, soft and sweet.

"Sandeep," I said. "You shouldn't say that."

But Becca laughed. Her laughter was almost as high and tinkly as the note Sandeep had just pressed. "How adorable," she said, and hugged Sandeep tighter.

He struggled a bit. "Juice," he said, looking at Rakel.

"Rakel, bring him the juice," Becca said. "This is my little friend, Sandeep, and his. . . ." She looked at me.

"Sister. Sort of," I said.

"Sandeep and his sort-of-sister, Poppy. This is Rakel."

Rakel's nostrils almost closed. She held the jar toward Sandeep, but not close enough for him to reach. "Do not spill on piano," she said sternly, fixing her eyes on him.

"Here," I said. "I'll hold him while he drinks," and I lifted him out of Becca's arms. For one second, I imagined that she wasn't letting go, just like she'd held on to my hand that fraction of a second too long on the street the other day. I had to give a tiny tug. But as Sandeep came into my arms, I heard my mother's voice, loud and clear in my head, telling me I was over-reacting again. I took the juice from Rakel and sat down on the sofa, with Sandeep on my lap, and held the jar of apple juice to his lips.

The couch seemed overstuffed and yet firm, almost like the cushions were tightly filled with feathers. The fabric was faded but beautiful – big red flowers on a yellow background. I looked around while Sandeep drank. There were lots of chairs, also big and cushiony, with similar patterns of flowers. The main color was faded yellow. The name of this kind of fabric suddenly came to me. *Chintz*. The walls were lined with paint-ings – mostly soft watercolors – in plain wood frames, and there were vases of flowers on a lot of the tables.

Books were lined neatly in open bookcases, and were also in symmetrical piles on small tables and cabinets and even on the top of the piano. There were photos everywhere – some color, some black-and-white – glossy, with signatures in the corners, and also lots of rugs, fringed, their patterns faded, overlapping each other on the hardwood floor. The whole room had a wonderfully comfortable feel, like one of those old English drawing rooms in ancient mystery movies about Sherlock Holmes or Miss Marple. And it was cool. Lovely and cool.

Rakel cleared her throat, a gruff grunt.

Sandeep drained the jar in a series of gulps. I held the jar toward Rakel. "Thanks," I said, then stood up, keeping a firm grip on Sandeep. "We'd better be going." I glanced at Rakel.

"Must you?" Becca said.

"Yes, Miss Becca," Rakel answered. "You will be overtired."

Miss Becca? Who is this old woman?

"All right," Becca said, with a put-on pout. "But I'll just walk them out. Could you pass me my hat, Poppy? On the table beside you."

As I reached for the hat, a large straw hat like the kind women wear to summer weddings, I noticed a basket beside the table. It was an old wicker basket, and in it were an assortment of beautiful plush animals – I could see parts of an elephant, a bird, a lion, and a

103

monkey on the top. They all were clean and plump and new-looking, the satiny ribbons around their necks in perfect bows.

"The sun is so damaging to one's skin," Becca said, putting on her hat and rolling down her sleeves. "And I really can't take a chance on being bitten by anything. I swell up terribly, even from a mosquito bite. The evenings are almost intolerable with these summer mosquitoes."

"Umm-hmmm," I said, glancing back at the basket of stuffed toys. Hadn't Rakel just said, "There are no children here"?

ELEVEN

Sandeep and I followed Becca through the patio door.

"Before you leave," she said, "come and see my garden."

"Rown and rown," Sandeep said.

"Do you like flowers?" Becca asked.

"I guess," I said. Mom had always made me help her with her vegetable garden plus all the flowers she planted.

Becca took me around the yard, pointing out more rosebushes, her perennial bed, her cutting bed, and her rockery. I basically said yeah, and that's pretty, and made other non-committal murmurings. Sandeep was getting heavy, and the bottom of his shorts felt damp, even with all the equipment I'd put on him.

"And of course there are the trees," Becca said. "I love my trees. Especially this one. This is my very special tree." She went toward that huge old tree whose branches Sandeep and I had been lying under in Linnea's yard. With no warning, she put one foot on the lowest branch, then swung herself up, climbing a few thick branches until she was over my head.

I was amazed that she could climb so easily. She wasn't that young, plus she seemed weak and, well, fragile. The clear, almost transparent, look of her skin, and the slow, deliberate way she walked – coupled with the fact that the first time I'd seen her she was fainting – made me realize that she probably wasn't in great health.

"I love to sit up here and think," Becca called down. "Ever since I was a girl, this has been my favorite place."

"You've lived here all your life?" I asked, looking up, shading my eyes with one hand.

She didn't answer for a moment. "On and off," she said. "One must go where the work is."

"Right," I said. "The acting."

"Yes," she said. She ran her hand up the old bark beside her. "But this is my true home." She plucked at the gold leaf on the chain around her neck, her hand closing on it. "Someone gave this to me once. He told me it was so that, when I couldn't be near my tree, I could still feel close." She lifted it to her lips and kissed it. "Sometimes I think of myself as a tree fairy," she said, letting the leaf fall. It settled against her pale skin as if magnetized.

"A tree fairy?" She was definitely bizarre.

"Fairy, nymph, what have you. Yes, this is my true home. I belong to this tree."

There was the sound of a door slamming in the next yard.

"Okay," I said. "I really should get going."

"Oh, look, it's Mac," Becca said. "Mac," she called. "Up here. Do come closer. Come and meet my guests."

The bushes parted, and a boy stepped through.

"Oh, hi," he said, a surprised look on his face.

"Hi," I said back. Sandeep started digging in my ear with his finger. I pulled his hand away.

"Go walk, Poppy," he said. "Go for walk."

Becca was watching Mac's face. "You know my friend Poppy?" she asked.

"No," I said.

"Last night," the boy said. "I saw you at my place."

"Your place?"

He waved in the direction of Linnea's house. "You were just leaving. I was coming home."

"Oh. Oh, yeah." The guy with the helmet hair and the safari suit. I couldn't believe this was the same guy. His hair was normal-looking now, cool even, and he was wearing jeans and a T-shirt. I tried to stop Sandeep from climbing up my chest. "We just saw each other. Last night," I called up to Becca, feeling somehow ridiculous. Sandeep stopped climbing abruptly, and sat still. Too still. His face was twisted in concentration, and color was starting up in it like a warming lava lamp.

Not now, Sandeep, I begged, silently. *Please, not now.* I moved a little further back from the boy. That's all I needed. Sandeep filling his diaper at this very moment.

"Well, this is Poppy, my new friend, and the little one is Sandeep," Becca said. "This is my neighbor — Mac. He's been looking after the yard for me this summer. He's wonderful with living things — not with just cutting the grass and trimming hedges and bushes, but also with the flowers. He has hands that make living things blossom and thrive. A perfect job for such hands."

Becca must have a thing for hands. Mac scraped at the ground with his foot, and his face was a similar shade to Sandeep's. I tried to see the amazing hands, but he had shoved them into his pockets. "So you're baby-sitting again?" he asked.

How does he know I'm always stuck with Sandeep? "Yeah," I said, my voice rising at the end so the word was a question.

"Tanner told me, this morning, about the girl with red hair and the happy name who read him *The Runaway Bunny* twenty-eleven times."

Mac. This is Linnea's brother, the one who likes salt and vinegar chips and Greek mythology.

"Now he'll never be satisfied with my one time again." Mac smiled, then looked at his watch. His left eye-tooth lapped over the front tooth, but his teeth were the whitest I've ever seen. "I've got to get to work, Ms. Jell."

"Could you come by, say, Monday?" she asked. "I'd like you to do some weeding. Everything grows so quickly in this warm weather, especially the weeds."

"Sure. I finish work early on Monday, at two. I'll come as soon as I get home. Hey," he said, looking at me, "is that your stroller in our yard?"

"Yeah. I was bringing Sandeep to play with Tanner, but they weren't home, and . . ." I stopped. There was no point in explaining the whole thing. "We're just leaving, so I'll come through and get it."

Sandeep smiled. "All done," he said.

I closed my eyes for a second. "Thank you for Sandeep's juice," I said to Becca.

She climbed down. "Will you come and visit again?" she asked. Her eyes, beneath the wide brim of her hat, were big, and there was something else. Almost a begging look.

"Um, well, maybe," I said.

"Do come. Please." She looked at me, her head slightly tilted to the side. "Aren't you the girl who likes acting?"

I nodded. A terrible smell was coming from the vicinity of Sandeep's shorts.

Becca clapped her hands together. "Well, then, that's perfect. I can show you all my scrapbooks. The posters and handbills from various shows. I've also done movies, and television."

I didn't say I know, I know about the one movie and the commercials. "Okay," I said, instead, edging toward the bushes.

"Adieu," Becca said.

Mac parted the bushes for me, and I had to step past him.

"Thanks," I said, with my head down. *What if he thinks the awful smell is me?*

"No problem. See you, Ms. Jell," he said, over his shoulder.

I settled Sandeep in his stroller, handing Didi to him, while Mac unlocked a bike from the back step. He walked beside me, along the side of the house and onto the street in the front. I could see, out of the corner of my eye, that the hair at the back of his neck was damp, as if he'd just had a shower. I think I smelled soap, even with Sandeep's dirty diaper smell clogging my nostrils.

"So how do you know her?" he asked. "Ms. Jell."

"I just met her today," I said. "By accident. Well, actually I met her before. Sort of. That was by accident, too. I don't really know her." *Could I sound any more clueless?*

Mac nodded as if he didn't notice anything wrong with my explanation. "She's a pretty sad case. All alone, with that old crone telling her what to do all day."

"Who is she? She calls Becca *Miss* Becca. It's so bizarre."

"I know. I guess she looks after Ms. Jell, or something."

"And is Becca always like this? I mean, she just seems off somehow. She was telling me that she's a tree fairy."

"A tree fairy?"

"Or tree nymph. I think that's what she said."

Mac stopped. "I'm into mythology," he said.

I know, I thought, but didn't say anything. I didn't want him to think I'd been checking out his things last night.

"They're called hamadryads." He got on his bike.

"Hamadryads?"

He pedaled beside me, slowly. I walked faster, and Sandeep gave a tiny squeal of pleasure, kicking his heels against the footrest.

"Yeah. In Greek mythology, there were these nymphs that lived in the forests. Each one had her own special tree." We got to the curb and waited while a garbage truck rumbled by. I bent over, making a big deal of tucking Didi into the stroller so I could take a good look at Mac without him noticing me staring. He was only a bit taller than me. His hair glinted in the sun, chestnut brown, with veins of rich dark gold streaked through it.

"My mother's in Greece right now," I said. I didn't want him to leave yet. I saw that his eyes were green, with the same dark gold glints that were in his hair.

"I'd love to get there someday." He pushed his bike off the curb, balancing on one foot on the road.

"So what happens?" I asked. "With these hama . . . hama what?"

"Dryads," he said, looking down at Sandeep. "Hamadryads." He pedaled in a circle in front of me. "Like I said, they live in the tree for as long as the tree lives." He lifted his hand in a wave. "See you," he said, and started down the road.

"And then what?" I called after him.

He looked over his shoulder at me.

"What happens to them? The hamadryads?"

"When the tree dies," Mac said, his voice getting fainter as he moved farther from me, "the hamadryad dies."

TWELVE

Dad was in the kitchen when I came in, pulling Sandeep by the hand. "What are you doing home?" I asked, depositing Sandeep beside Dad.

"I just came home to check on Calypso," he said, concentrating on spooning a gucky-looking mixture onto doughy rounds. "She hasn't been feeling well these last few weeks. The carpets can wait."

I thought about the people waiting for those rolled-up logs of carpets in the back of the van.

"You're just in time for lunch," he said. "I'm making garbanzo bean wraps. I want to make sure Calypso has something nourishing to eat. Sometimes she skips meals, when she's busy."

"Oh, yum," I said, rolling my eyes at him. "How did you guess garbanzo beans are what I've been craving?" My sarcasm was always lost on Dad. He didn't even glance up from the counter. "And Sandeep's got a dirty diaper. It's all yours." *Dad's so thrilled to play kissy-kissy with Sandeep. Let him change his stinky diaper.* "I'm really sweaty. I'm taking a bath."

I grabbed some clean clothes from my room and pushed the bathroom door open. There was Calypso, larger than life, emerging from the tub, dripping like some hideous and bloated sea witch.

"Oh, my God," I said, slamming the door.

"It's all right; come on in," Calypso called. She opened the door, still naked, toweling her long hair. "I'm finished." She bent forward, wrapping the towel around her head turban-style, then straightened. She rubbed her hands over her belly. "I had a wonderful meeting with my midwife, but I needed to cool off. My internal thermostat is a little higher when I'm pregnant."

It was a grotesque sight. Her belly button stuck out like the bottom of a pogo stick. I didn't think the human body was capable of expanding that much. Her skin was lined with squiggly streaks of red that I knew must be stretch marks; all I could think of was fatty uncooked bacon.

"I'll just wait in my room," I mumbled, backing up, then turning and trying to stroll, composed, down the hall.

"Don't be embarrassed," Calypso called after me. "I'm celebrating my body. You should, too. Your body is the temple of —" but I slammed my bedroom door before I could hear what she had to say about my body. From now on I was knocking.

🌳

If only she were the stepmother of fairy tales — the wicked, scheming old hag. But she's not any of those things – not wicked, not scheming, and she's definitely not a hag. She's just, well, Calypso is . . . Calypso. She's big, not just because she's pregnant, but big in a tall strong earth-mother way. Dark brown eyes – almond-shaped – beautiful smooth fair skin, and that hair – so much of it, straight and shiny, right down to her waist. I wish I could hate her, but actually I can't figure out how I feel about her.

She's the total opposite of my mother. In body and in mind. I've never seen my mother's body in less than a bathing suit, and I realize now that I've never even had a glimpse of her mind.

"Poppy?" It was Calypso, outside my bedroom door.

"What?" I called. I was in the rocking chair, cross-legged, with both my *M* Book and my scrapbook in my lap. My scrapbook held programs from the school plays I'd been in, as well as a few community newspaper write-ups about the couple of productions I'd been in with my Teen Act courses at the Theater for Young People.

"Can I come in?"

"Only if you're dressed," I said.

There was a moment's silence. "Of course I'm dressed," she answered, opening the door. She had a wide-toothed comb in her hand. "I'm sorry if I upset you," she said. "I know that you're not used to our lifestyle. Eric told me how uptight your mother is, but I keep forgetting."

"She's not that uptight," I said. "At least not anymore. After all, she did run away with a poet."

Calypso didn't say anything for a few seconds, then sat on the bed and combed her hair. "I love being pregnant. Nothing feels as good to me as doing this. Growing a baby. It feels like it's the one thing I was meant to do."

"What about your quilts?" I asked. "You like doing that."

"Oh, of course. But to create life . . . well, there's no other feeling. I remember my own conception, you know."

For just a few seconds, when she was apologizing to me, I had a moment of warming up to Calypso. She should have stopped while she was ahead.

I couldn't think of a thing to say.

"It was the summer of love, Poppy," she told me. She put down the comb and started caressing her bulging abdomen in slow, regular circles. I don't think she was even conscious of it. "The summer of the hip and homeless, of magic bus trips, and of love. Love both profound and frivolous. Have you ever been in love?"

I wasn't expecting that, but at least she considered me old enough to be in love, unlike Mom, who had never asked about my love life. Not that I had one, really. "I guess not," I said. I had wanted to be in love with someone for at least the last year. Kieran Wasylik was my best option, although he hadn't been quite as enthusiastic as I wanted him to be.

"It was at Woodstock," she went on. "My mother and father fell in love there, and I was created out of that love. My first memory is of a gentle *poof*, like the puff of smoke a magician makes. And then . . . I was."

"Was?"

"I became," Calypso said.

I stared down at my scrapbook, unable to look at her. I was surrounded by craziness. Cat hair balls, tree nymphs, and memories from the womb.

Calypso patted the sides of her bulge. "I hope you remember it, too, little one," she said, looking down, then started the circles again. "I could feel the love surrounding me. I felt tiny, but huge, at the same time."

"I get that feeling when I have a fever," I said, hoping that would stop the conversation. But Calypso didn't even seem to hear me.

"I never felt that kind of love again. That all-encompassing safe love. Not until I met your father."

I tried again. "So which was your parents' love? You said it was the summer of love, profound and frivolous. What kind of love did your parents have?"

"Hmmm," Calypso said, her hands stopping in midswirl. "I would have to say both." Her hands started again. "Because they loved each other passionately, but for a very short time."

"Sort of like Romeo and Juliet."

Calypso shook her head. "No. There was nothing frivolous about Romeo and Juliet's love. Because of it, they both died."

I nodded. "More like profound and tragic."

"Exactly. My parents met there, at Woodstock, and they never saw each other again," Calypso went on. "But my mother assured me that the three days of love with my father were the most profound in her life."

I pulled my *M* Book on top of the scrapbook, looking down at the glossy picture I'd glued onto the cover. "Did you ever try to find him? Your dad?"

Even though I wasn't looking, I could tell that Calypso's hands had stopped. "No. My mother didn't even know his last name."

There was a different movement. I looked up at her, and saw that she was playing with her comb, running the teeth of it over her palm.

"Does it bother you?"

"That I didn't know my father?" She raised her head, and I saw her eyes flicker. "No," she finally said. "My mother was a totally cool person. We had a good life. Why?"

I shrugged.

"Are you wondering about your real father?" she asked me.

"Not really. But I do think about my real mother. I really want to find her. Meet her."

"Why?" she asked again.

I tried to find the right words. "I feel . . . unfinished. Like I'm not real yet. And I can't be, until I find out about her."

"Not real?"

"The only time I feel that I'm complete is when I'm on the stage. When I'm someone else. Because then I know exactly who I'm supposed to be, what to think, what to feel. But when I come off the stage, and get rid of my costume and makeup, I don't feel real."

I didn't want to look at her when I was telling her this stuff. I'd never told anyone. But since Calypso was already a little off-the-wall, she seemed an okay person to tell.

She nodded, then opened her mouth, but closed it again. After a few seconds, she said, "I do know what you mean."

We sat there. I could hear Dad talking to Sandeep, then Dad's footsteps on the stairs, and the closing of Sandeep's door.

"Calypso?" I said.

"Hmmm?" She smiled at me.

"I want to find her. My real mom. She might still be here, in Winnipeg." I tensed, waiting for her to tell me not to be silly, or that it was a bad idea.

But Calypso just nodded, then ran the comb down her cheek. "What do you think you should do first?"

Okay. She isn't going to help me, but she isn't going to try and talk me out of it. "I know I can't find anything out, legally, until I'm eighteen."

"Yes. Locating a birth parent is lumped with the other hugely important aspects of life, like voting or drinking."

I didn't smile at her attempted joke. "I know."

Calypso kept running the comb up and down her cheek. "So there's really nothing you can actually do."

The more I thought about it, and talked about it, first to Dad and now Calypso, the more hopeless it sounded. "Well, I could just walk around, and stare into everyone's face, and look for a woman who looks like she could be my mother," I said, suddenly mad at Calypso, and even more mad at myself, for actually thinking that by coming to Winnipeg I *could* find her in exactly that way. "If I was born at the Misericordia, then my mother probably lived around here. Maybe she still does. It makes sense, doesn't it?" I demanded, even though I knew I was really reaching.

"Um-hmmm," Calypso murmured. "Sure."

"Who knows," I said, my voice getting louder. "Maybe our paths have already crossed. It could happen."

When Calypso didn't make a sound, I said it again, even louder, as if Calypso were arguing with me. "It could happen. Strange things happen all the time. Why not this?" As I looked down again, I studied my hands, thinking of Becca's hands on the piano keys. We did have the same shape of fingers, long and slender, the nails really oval, and the moon on the thumbnail showing more than on the rest of the fingers.

"Why not?" she said.

Dad stuck his head in the doorway. "Why not what? What are you girls up to?" he asked.

"Nothing," I said, glancing at Calypso. She was smiling, in a lazy way, at my dad.

"Are you feeling a little better?" Dad asked. When Calypso nodded, he said, "I gave Sandeep some lunch, and put him down for his nap. I'm off on my next delivery." He set down his cowboy boots and stepped into one of them.

"Eric," Calypso said. "Not the boots. You know how they upset me."

"Alligator," Dad said, by way of explanation. "Some mean old gator lost his life to make my boots. At least ten years ago. I got my sneakers wet this morning, Calypso. Had to do a delivery on a street with a water main break. I don't have any choice."

"You always say that. You do have a choice. Throw them out."

Dad didn't answer, pulling his pant legs down over the boots. "Where'd you go this morning, Poppy? Sandeep told me some story about eggs and apple juice."

"We went to find Tanner, but he wasn't there," I said, getting out of the rocking chair. "We were talking to the woman in the house next door." I didn't need to give

him all the details about how I fell asleep and lost
Sandeep. "You grew up in this area, right?"

"A few streets from here," he said.

"Did you ever know anyone who lived on
Palmerston? In the big houses?"

Dad straightened. "Not really. We used to think of
them as the rich people. I had a paper route there for a few
years, though. I remember one house giving me a whole
five dollars for a tip one Christmas. That was a lot when I
was a kid."

"What about the house Linnea stays in?"

"You know it, Eric," Calypso said. "The big yellow
brick one."

Dad nodded.

"So do you know the one next door?" I asked. "It's
sort of the same shape, but not as tall, and it's brick,
too. Red."

"The one next door." He put his thumb and index
finger on one end of his mustache, and twirled. "Nope.
Can't say I do."

"Think, Dad. It's a little spooky, but neat, too. It has
a black wrought-iron fence in the front."

Dad looked at the ceiling, still twirling his mustache.
"Wrought-iron fence?"

"Yeah."

"I know which one you're talking about. Yup. There
was a girl lived there; I remember now. A pale skinny girl.
When I'd go to collect every two weeks, she'd stand in the

hall, half behind a big curtain that draped over another doorway, and just stare at me. I remember that she'd always be wearing a uniform, a kilt or something, with a white blouse and tie. She must have gone to Balmoral Hall, or St. Mary's. One of the private schools."

"That could be her. Was her name Becca? Becca Jell?"

Dad shook his head. "Can't remember the name. But there was a strange story about that house. What was it now?" He frowned for an instant, then shrugged. "Nope. Can't remember. Maybe it'll come to me later. Why?"

"That's who I was talking to this morning – the woman who lives there. Her name is Becca Jell, and she's really bizarre. Actually, she's an actress."

"Oh," Calypso said. "That's the woman Linnea has talked about. She was in a movie once."

"Becca Jell," Dad said. "The name doesn't ring any bells. Gotta go. See you at supper," he added, giving Calypso a peck on the cheek. "I left a couple of bean wraps on the kitchen table for you gals."

"Thanks, Eric," Calypso said, pulling her fingers through her hair, separating it into three thick strands. "I'm going to spend Sandeep's nap time sewing. I should be finished the hand-stitching on the quilt for your boss' wife this week. The Romance of the Roses pattern. You can tell him."

"Okeydokey," Dad said. He clattered down the uncarpeted stairs in his cowboy boots. I heard the door open, but didn't hear it close.

"Poppy," he called.

I went to the top of the stairs and bent over so I could see him. He was standing in the doorway, holding the outer screen door open by the handle. A cabbage butterfly flew in past him and lit on the newel post at the end of the banister. It fluttered there, like a tiny white living bow on a round wooden head.

"I just remembered something. About the people who lived in the house."

"What?"

"There was some trouble, later, when I was older. Some trouble, and someone died. Or maybe just ran off. What was it, now?"

"Dad, think."

He stood there another few seconds. "That's all that comes to me, right now, but I'll keep working on it. The mind's a funny thing, isn't it? It was Calypso mentioning that pattern, and the roses, that did it. It was something about roses." He tapped his temple. "Put a penny in and you never know what you might get in return," he said, then went through the door, letting go of the handle. It swung closed with a quiet *whump*, and the draft of warm air it created lifted the cabbage butterfly. It rose with the small current, up, up the stairs toward me, silently, effortlessly, a plain and ghostly version of its flamboyant monarch sister.

THIRTEEN

I had strange mixed-up dreams about the people on Palmerston Avenue all night. Linnea and Tanner and Mr. Hartley. Mac. Rakel and Becca.

I wondered when I'd get to see them again. Especially Becca. And Mac. There was definitely something about Mac. I kept thinking about his clean soapy smell, and his hair, damp against the back of his neck.

The next afternoon I ended up seeing him again, but it was a disaster. There are moments in one's life that are too humiliating for words.

It started in the morning – Saturday morning in the raspberry house – and the day stretched out in front of me like a prison sentence. At least Dad and Calypso let me sleep in for a change, and I didn't get up until after eleven.

"Is the washing machine fixed yet?" I asked Calypso as I came downstairs and into the kitchen. I only had about two things left to wear that weren't dirty.

"Someone's coming out around five to have a look at it," she called back. "But before he comes," she said, as she took a sponge mop out of the broom closet, "we're going to a street festival, downtown in the Exchange District. There'll be all kinds of acts, your dad says – improv, open mikes, a poetry slam, magicians – you name it. He can finish work early, and keep the van until six, so he just phoned to say he'll pick us up soon. You'll like that, won't you? Your dad said you'd like that kind of thing." Her expression was so eager that it made me, for just a moment, feel a nudge of pity. And her face was puffy. She didn't look that good.

"I guess," I said.

"Have something to eat then, and keep Sandeep busy for an hour while I try to straighten up a little, okay?"

"Watch him again?" I said, looking down at Sandeep playing on the kitchen floor with some plastic mixing bowls.

"Again?" he said to a green bowl, turning it upside down and trying to stand on it. He scooted across the floor on his bare bottom, putting the smallest bowl, a red one, into his potty.

But Calypso didn't seem to hear me, and walked heavily toward the living room, dragging the mop behind her. I saw that her ankles and feet were swollen, puffing up over the edges of her Birkenstock sandals. She wasn't whistling.

I sat at the kitchen table, drinking a glass of orange juice and reading the *Seventeen* magazine I'd brought with me. Sandeep kept fooling around with the bowls.

In a while I heard Dad talking to Calypso in the other room. "You ready to go?" he asked me, coming into the kitchen. I was still wearing my boxers and T-shirt.

"Just have to change," I said.

"Where's my boy?" he called. "Sandeep?"

I looked at the floor and the bowls. He was gone. Again. He couldn't have gone out to the backyard; Calypso always kept the screen door hooked for that very reason.

"I think he's upstairs," I said, bluffing, and ran up.

"Sandeep," I said in a loud whisper, passing my room. "Where are you?" I glanced into his room, and the bathroom, and Dad and Calypso's. "Sandeep," I said again, low, under my breath. "You come out. Where are you?"

There was silence, then a little voice said, from my room, "Sandee yook at Poppy's toys."

I marched into my room, and there he was, half behind the door, with a pile of my makeup spread around him. "You bad boy," I said, pulling him away. "You're not supposed to take my things."

"Not bad boy," he said, his mouth getting that square look that means he's going to cry.

"Okay, okay," I whispered quickly, hugging him with one arm, "okay, you're not a bad boy. Don't start crying." I was supposed to be watching him, after all. His mouth relaxed. "Now go find your mommy. Get some pants on. We're going out," I told him.

As I heard him going down the stairs, I opened my closet door and reached for one of my last clean pairs of shorts and tops, in their neat pile on the floor. "Ewww!"

I half shrieked, jerking my hand away. They were wet. Wet and soggy. I stood there for a minute, digesting what had happened, then marched to the top of the stairs.

"SANDEEP!" I bellowed, my voice echoing through the house. In a minute both Dad and Calypso's faces peered up at me. "That little brat peed on my clothes!" I yelled. "I can't stand this! This place is making me crazy!"

❦

Of course I wasn't going to go to the street festival because I had nothing to wear until the washing machine was fixed. I couldn't even pull anything out of my dirty clothes, because I'd thrown wet towels in with them and everything was smelly and damp.

I shouldn't have listened to her, but Calypso talked me into wearing a pair of her prepregnancy-but-still-baggy shorts and this stupid, equally baggy T-shirt that said NOT ALL QUILTERS ARE SQUARES. I knew I looked like a complete fool, but who would I see, anyway? And who would see me? Plus I couldn't bear the thought of killing a Saturday afternoon in the hot house, with three shedding overweight cats, no television worth watching, no CD player and only scratchy old blues records to listen to.

So, wearing the totally uncool clothes, I went along, walking through the crowds at the festival, trailing after Calypso pushing Sandeep in his stroller and Dad with his guitar slung across his back. I watched as Dad put his arm across Calypso's shoulders, whispering something to her, and she threw back her head and laughed, and the sound of her laugh made me feel left out and lonely for something I couldn't name. They looked so . . . complete. They were this family, and there I was, alone, a few steps behind, unrecognizable in middle-aged clothes.

Where was the cool person I had been in Vancouver, wearing cool clothes from a cool shop, surrounded by cool friends, hanging out in places where other cool people hung out? That Poppy was gone, lost in mirrors that were warped, eating food that was alien, and now swimming in clothes that were foreign.

"Oh, look," Calypso said, stopping. "It's Mac! Hi, Mac! Over here."

I froze. *Please. No.* I tried for a casual, totally uninterested smile, but my mouth wouldn't work right.

Mac was coming toward us. And beside him was this incredibly gorgeous girl.

"How are you, Mac?" Calypso said. "Eric, you remember Mac, Linnea's brother. And have you met Eric's daughter, Poppy?"

"Yeah, sure," Mac said, his smile open. "This is Alissa. Alissa, this is Eric, and Calypso, Poppy, and the little guy is Sandeep." He had pointed at us, one by one. "They're friends of my sister's."

Alissa looked at me, at my hair, and then my T-shirt, and then my shorts. "Hi," she said. Did I hear held-back laughter in that word? Her dark blonde hair, in a high ponytail, shone. Just the right number of hairs had come loose around her face, framing it in charming wispy strands. Her eyelashes were long and darkened with mascara, and her full lips were peachy and glossy.

I licked my own dry bottom lip. I hadn't bothered to wear any makeup. *Quick. Who can I be?*

Alissa daintily picked up one of the tiny straps of her tank top, and settled it over her shoulder.

I was ballooning, growing into an elephant with a huge, wrinkly, ill-fitting skin of clothes, right before their eyes.

"Have you caught any of the acts?" Mac asked.

"We just got here," Calypso said. "But Eric's going to do some playing."

What? He's playing? Why did I come?

"There's a stage farther down where you can perform," she went on. "Eric's arranged with a sax player to do a few numbers."

I can't think of a character. My mind is a blank.

"Maybe we'll catch it," Mac said, glancing at Alissa. "Have you got time?"

Please don't have time.

Alissa lazily lifted her hairless arm, looking at her watch. "I don't think so," she said, barely opening her flawless, glistening, peachy lips. She looked at me again.

My armpits were wet. There were probably huge pit stains on the elephant-skin T-shirt.

"Sorry," Mac said, smiling first at Dad, and then at me.

"No problem," Dad said.

Everyone said good-bye, and then Calypso looked at me. "You didn't tell me you'd met Mac, Poppy."

I just nodded. A few days ago I had dismissed Mac as too uncool for someone like me. Now I was too uncool for anyone. The emptiness inside me was getting bigger and bigger, stretching to match my clothes.

What is happening?

I need to find her.

FOURTEEN

Nothing could be worse than Saturday, so even though Sunday was long and dreary, with Dad twanging his guitar and playing his endless records, at least there was no way I could be humiliated if I stayed inside.

But by Monday afternoon I knew I had to get out of the raspberry house. All morning I'd helped Calypso with piles of laundry that had accumulated in front of the now-fixed washing machine in the damp old basement, attempted to clear up the cluttered kitchen, and tried to keep Sandeep out of trouble. I hadn't done so well in that department. Sandeep had accidentally slammed the tip of T-Bone's tail in a door, flushed my favorite eyeliner down the toilet, and dumped a cup of sand from his sandbox into the blender.

I wanted to go to Palmerston Avenue. I wanted to be inside that cool beautiful room with the piano and flowers and serenity. Right after lunch, when Calypso went to lie down with Sandeep, I got on my bike.

Becca *had* invited me to come back. She hadn't been specific about the day or time. I got off my bike in front of the Jell house, and walked it around to the backyard. As I passed the window I knew was the dining room, there was movement. I turned my head quickly, but it was only the curtain swaying, as if someone had walked by it.

Rounding the corner of the house, I saw Becca and Mac. Becca was standing with her back against her tree. Mac was crouching near her, pulling weeds from among the planted pansies and pinwheel petunias. He had his shirt off, and each time he reached forward to grab another weed, the muscles in his back rippled.

I could see Becca's mouth moving, talking to Mac, although I couldn't hear anything from this far away. It was a normal scene, but there was something about the way Becca was leaning against the tree, something about the way she had her hands behind her back, the way she was tossing her hair around, that looked wrong. I stood there, watching.

Becca spoke again, and Mac looked up and answered, a tight smile on his face.

Becca laughed — a long, trilling laugh. She brought one pale hand out from behind her and put it on her throat, and then let it slide down until it was resting just over the little gold key and leaf. She said something else.

Mac looked down at the ground in front of him again, ripping out weeds and long pieces of grass with hard, short jerks.

I saw him shake his head.

Then Becca reached out with the toe of her soft shoe and touched the back of Mac's calf, just once. Lightly.

Mac froze, his hand in midair, still clutching a fistful of spiky green.

"Becca!" I called. I hadn't meant to shout like that. "Hi. I came to see you." I walked across the broad expanse of green.

At the sound of my voice Mac jumped up, shoving the weeds into a garbage bag beside him on the ground.

Becca turned to me, her eyes wide and innocent. "Poppy. What a lovely surprise."

"I was just riding by, and thought I'd stop and say hello." I didn't look at Mac. Even though I was wearing my own clothes, I knew he was seeing me as he had on Saturday. How could he not?

"I'm glad you have," Becca said. She leaned over and plucked one of the pinwheel petunias, then smiled down at its starry, red and white throat.

Mac was pulling on his T-shirt. While his head was covered, I took the opportunity to stare at his torso, looking away the next second as the shirt slid off his face. "I guess that's it for today then, Ms. Jell," he said.

"Please." Becca twirled the petunia against her cheek. "It's Becca. Don't make me tell you again, Nigel, you naughty boy."

Why did she call him Nigel?

Mac concentrated on gathering up the bag, tying a tight knot at the top. He didn't correct her. "So I'll be back on Thursday, then," he said. "To cut the grass."

"Oh, no. That's too long. Those rosebushes in the front will need attention before that. Could you come tomorrow? Anytime at all, tomorrow. Please?" she smiled, a big open smile. "For me?"

I thought I might gag.

"I don't start until noon tomorrow," Mac said. "I guess I could come before that."

"That would be lovely," Becca replied. "I shall expect you . . ." She paused, as if checking a mental calendar, "Shall we say about tenish?"

Scarlett O'Hara all the way. Next she'd be telling him she'd have a cool mint julep waiting for him.

"Okay," Mac said, then finally looked at me. "How're you doing, Poppy? Have a good time at the festival?"

"Yeah. Yeah," I repeated, nodding my head, desperately thinking of a character I could play. *Nothing.* "You?"

"Good." He nodded, too.

We were like those pecking birds on a stick, the ones whose heads just keep bobbing, senselessly. There was a heavy uncomfortable sensation. I knew that for me it was partly embarrassment at witnessing Becca flirting with Mac, but mostly my own humiliation at what Mac probably thought of me now. I could imagine him and Alissa laughing at me. The feeling hovered around us. It was almost as though it had substance — that I could reach out and touch it, like Becca had touched Mac's leg.

"So, do you go to school around here?" I asked, just something to break the weighty silence to show him that I didn't care what he thought of me.

"Yeah. Gordon Bell," he said, dropping his eyes. "Going into grade twelve. You?"

His eyes were brown. *Why had I thought they were green?* "I'm starting grade eleven this fall. But not here. Back in Vancouver. That's where I live."

He nodded.

I nodded back. We were starting the bird thing again.

Becca was silent. I glanced at her, but she was concentrating on the petunia.

"Okay. I'll see you, then," Mac said. "I've got to get to work."

"Mac works at World o' Pets on Portage Avenue," Becca said.

That explained the safari outfit I'd first seen him in. He was edging toward the bushes, like he couldn't wait to get away. I didn't blame him.

"Okay," he said, "Tomorrow, Ms. Jell." He lowered his eyes. "Becca." He said it quickly, mumbled, like the name didn't fit his tongue, but he knew he had no choice.

"Lovely," she answered, watching him leave through the opening in the bushes. Then she lowered herself onto a white iron bench near the tree. Beside the bench was a low, matching table. On it was a frosted glass pitcher of what looked like iced tea, and two of those delicate glasses I'd seen in the kitchen cupboards.

"Come and keep me company," she said, patting the spot on the bench beside her. "And have some iced tea." She filled one of the glasses. "I had Rakel bring it out for Mac, but he didn't want any. He's such a hard worker. Look. The ice hasn't even melted yet."

"No." I knew my "no" sounded as sulky as Sandeep's when Calypso told him it was time for his nap. Now I wish I hadn't come. *What did I expect? Why did seeing Becca flirt with Mac bother me so much — even though it embarrassed him? He obviously isn't interested in anything I have to say, anyway. He has Alissa.* "I don't feel like sitting," I said. "I've been sitting a lot today." I hadn't sat down once, running up and down stairs doing laundry and chasing Sandeep.

"Suit yourself," Becca said, taking a sip of her iced tea. Still holding the glass, she started humming. I recognized the tune. It was "Some Enchanted Evening." I hated that song. My mother used to sing it when she was doing housework.

All of a sudden everybody bugged me. Calypso, and my father, and Sandeep. Now Becca, for her ridiculous flirting with Mac. Even Mac bugged me, for letting Becca make a fool of him. And for Alissa.

Becca stopped humming, and played with the curlicue on the edge of the curved arm of the bench. "What's wrong?"

"Nothing."

"If this is an example of your acting talent, you disappoint me, Poppy."

"What do you mean?" I looked at the river.

"Well, if you want to portray the image that nothing is wrong, you're not acting it out very well. Let me guess." She laughed her little trilling laugh. "It's very clear, Poppy, my dear. I do believe you are jealous." She said it in her fake southern belle drawl. I hated that voice.

"I'm not jealous," I said. "What are you talking about? Jealous of what?"

"Oh, darling," Becca said, that simpering smile still on her face, "bravo. Well done." She set her glass on the table.

I looked at her. I wanted to say, "It's sickening, watching you flirt with Mac. You have to be close to twenty years older than him." But she could do anything she wanted in her own yard. And I was here as her guest. As long as I chose to stay, I had no right to say anything to her. Although it was hard to keep quiet.

"Come now, Poppy. Have some iced tea. Let's be done with all this scowling." She clapped her hands twice, and then opened them in front of her own face, as if she were a magician. "Everything is cleared away. We shall start our visit afresh. Tell me all about your day," she said, pouring iced tea into the second glass. She picked hers up again, but I left mine on the table.

"Nothing. Nothing happened. Just more dumb baby-sitting."

Becca's voice was suddenly serious. "He's lovely. Your little brother is beautiful. I don't know much about children, but obviously he adores you. There's such an age gap between you two. I'm sure you're almost like another mother to him."

I shook my head. "Not really. And he's only my half brother." I stopped. "In reality, he's nothing to me." I looked at my glass of iced tea.

"He's nothing to you?"

"It's a long story. I'm just visiting here. Like I told Mac, I live in Vancouver, but I came here to Winnipeg to . . ." I stopped. I didn't want to get into it. "My mother's in Greece. So I came here to stay with my father until she gets back. My father and his new family."

"And do you miss her? Your mother?"

I shrugged.

"But you must. The strongest bond, the most natural attachment, is between a mother and her child."

"Maybe. But she doesn't feel that attachment for me, so it's hard for me to feel it for her."

Becca shook her head. "I don't believe that. Not for one minute."

"What don't you believe? That she doesn't feel anything for me? Or that I don't feel anything for her?"

"Both," Becca said, firmly.

"How can you know? You just said you don't know much about kids. You never had any?" I thought of the basket of toys.

Becca suddenly brought her glass to her lips and took a long swallow. She paused, then drank again.

"One thing I do know is how to read people's faces."
She hadn't answered my question. "And your face, as the
saying goes, is an open book, my dear. You have a very
expressive face, and although you may think you're
hiding what you're feeling, you're not. What I see you
feeling is a sadness over your missing mother. And love
for her."

To my horror, I felt my eyes smarting. I looked up at
the branches of Becca's tree, swallowing and swallowing,
hoping to choke back the tears. Sometimes it worked.
"That's a pretty tree," I said, changing the subject. The
tree wasn't really pretty; so many of the leaves were
chewed and ragged, victims of worm ravage. "What
kind is it?"

"An elm. When a woman has a child," she said, not
seeming to realize that I didn't want to talk about my
mother, "the bond she feels for the life she created can
never be broken. She thinks about that child all the time,
wanting, more than anything, for the child to be happy.
And to be loved."

I looked down, away from the sad branches, and at
Becca. She was staring past me, a thoughtful expression
on her face.

"But that's just it," I said. "She's not my real mother.
I'm adopted. So there goes your theory. She didn't create
me, so she doesn't necessarily have those real mother
feelings toward me."

Becca blinked once, and there was a delay of maybe two seconds. Then her eyes swung toward me. "You were adopted?"

I nodded.

In the silence that followed, I could hear the chiming of a Dickee-Dee ice-cream bike somewhere out on Wolseley. The rhythmic barking of a dog. The dull roar of an outboard motor from the river.

Finally Becca spoke again. "Do you remember anything of your birth mother?"

"No. I was just tiny, a couple of weeks old, when I was adopted."

Becca was studying my hair. "I was motherless, too, for a while," she said. "Until Rakel came. She tried to fill the spot, but —"

"What happened to your mother?"

"She went away when I was a little girl. About the age of your brother. Between two and three."

"Why?"

"Grown-up reasons. That's all my father ever would say. He destroyed every single picture of her, so I don't even know what she looked like. 'Grown-up reasons, Rebecca,' my father would say. 'Nothing for you to worry about.'" She laughed, not her usual bubbling laugh, but a harsh bark. "Nothing for me to worry about." She got up and went toward the rosebushes. "Rakel still looks after me, the old dear," she said. "A bit too ferociously, I'm afraid. We all show love in different ways."

I followed her.

She bent down and picked up a pair of orange-handled clippers, lying half under a rosebush. "Nigel left the clippers out," she said. "They could rust." She was doing it again, calling Mac Nigel.

Becca opened and closed them, then halfheartedly snipped at a few of the longer branches in front of her. But a twig got jammed between the blades. Becca picked it out and threw it onto the ground, then opened and closed the clippers a few more times. There was a clean satisfying cutting sound as the short, curved blades opened and closed on the air in front of her.

"Do you remember her?" I asked. "Your mother?"

Becca nodded, looking at the rosebush. She reached out and ran her hand over the feathery new summer growth. "I used to think that my mother was a beautiful princess, with long, long hair. Like Rapunzel. I know it sounds unbelievable, because I was so young when she left, but I do have a memory of her."

"It doesn't sound unbelievable," I said. Calypso's memory of her conception was unbelievable. This wasn't. Wouldn't Sandeep remember something, some tiny thing, of Calypso, if he never saw her again?

"It's very hazy, almost surreal." Becca closed her eyes. "I can't see her features, just the pale oval of her face, but I can feel her hair against my cheek, soft, sweeping. And

I know it smelled good. I don't know what the smell was, but it was good. That's all." She opened her eyes, her hand still now, the fingertips just touching the edges of the leaves. There was a quiet calm look on her face. I didn't want to say anything to break this mood. But suddenly a squirrel chattered from a nearby tree, scolding, and Becca jumped, and the relaxed look vanished.

She made the barking sound that was supposed to be laughter again, and put her hand on her chest, as if it hurt. "I spent my whole childhood waiting for her to come back and rescue me."

"Rescue you? From what?"

Becca looked at the house. "From here. This place." She waved her arms around the yard. "And him – my father. From my life." She threw the clippers onto the ground, and pulled in a long, raspy breath, then another. She lifted her face and closed her eyes, breathing with difficulty. Then she crossed her arms over her chest and walked away from me, toward the house, her head down, leaning forward, her steps long and purposeful, like she was striding headfirst through a strong wind.

On the way she banged into the table, knocking over her glass of iced tea. It fell, hitting the grass soundlessly, the tea sloshing and the ice bouncing out.

But in spite of it being so fragile-looking, the glass didn't break.

FIFTEEN

I stood there for at least a full minute, then, realizing she wasn't coming back, went and picked up her glass. I left it on the table beside my own full one, got my bike, and wheeled it around the house. As I opened the front gate, Mac called to me. He was sitting on the front step of his house, wiping a pair of pruning shears with an oily rag. "Going home?"

"I guess so," I said.

"It's a weird scene sometimes, over there," he said. The awkwardness that had surrounded us in Becca's backyard didn't seem to exist here.

"Yeah. I don't get her. One minute she's chatting away, and the next she's off in some other world."

He stood and walked toward me. "What did she do now?"

"She got all philosophical about love, talking about her father and how her mother left her. And then she started to have an asthma attack."

"She's a pretty sad case," Mac said.

"Do you know if she ever had a kid?" I hadn't meant to ask that.

Mac shrugged, putting down the shears. "I've never seen anyone around except the old lady. And she's never said anything to me about kids. Why?"

"I don't know. Just . . . there are these toys in her house, and . . . I can't explain it. It's just a feeling." I looked at the shears on the step beside Mac. "And what's the deal with her calling you Nigel?"

He shrugged. "She's done it every once in a while, right from the first time she called me over and asked if she could hire me to work in her yard." He seemed so different now, relaxed; it was much easier to talk to him away from Becca's yard.

"So how come you live with your sister?" I asked him.

"Things weren't so good at home." His eyes were darker now. "And Linnea needed help – with the rent, and with Tanner. So I moved in with her last fall. It works out pretty well for both of us."

"You've lived here for almost a year, then?"

"Yeah. Tanner's a really great little guy. And Linnea and I have always been okay together. It's not too bad. The old guy – Mr. Hartley – runs the place like a boarding school, but the price is right." He looked up at the house, and I looked, too.

"That's what Linnea said."

"What about you?" he asked. "How're you making out with Calypso? Linnea thinks she's great."

"She's okay. Just . . . different than what I'm used to. So is my dad, and their whole house." I ran my hand over my handlebars.

He nodded. "I like her name. Calypso. Is it from *The Odyssey*?"

"What?"

Mac shrugged. "Sorry. It's the mythology thing again. You haven't heard of *The Odyssey*?"

Somehow I knew he didn't mean *Space Odyssey*. I shook my head.

"It's a heavy old classic. Takes forever to read, but you can get caught up in it. There's this Greek warrior, Odysseus, and he's on a quest to get home from the Trojan War."

His eyes were lighter now. As I watched him talk, he shifted so that the sun hit his face, and his eyes sort of transformed. They were green, like I had seen yesterday.

I guess it's a bit like blushing, the eye thing, giving away how he was feeling. His eyes were obviously hazel, but they turned green when he was feeling okay, and then when he didn't feel so great, got darker, taking on the brown tone. I tried to go back to the story he was telling me.

"On this long voyage home, Odysseus stops at an island, and this beautiful woman – whose name is Calypso – enchants him. He stays there with her for seven years, until he comes to his senses and sets out for home again."

"Does he get there?"

"Yeah. And when he does, his family is still waiting for him. They haven't given up. It's a good story, but like I said, it's really long. It takes perseverance to get through it. Once you start, you can't give up."

"Sort of like Odysseus. And his family."

"Yeah. It really is a story about the search for home; trying to find your way home. About having faith in yourself, and the people who really love you."

We were both quiet, but it wasn't uncomfortable. It seemed a profound moment. I don't remember talking to Kieran about anything quite so dramatic. In fact, at this moment, I couldn't recall Kieran ever saying anything remotely interesting. Actually, we didn't talk a lot, but he was great at kissing. I suddenly thought of kissing Mac, and my face and neck got hot. Then I thought of him kissing Alissa, and immediately went cold.

"So how long will your mother be on her Greek island?" he asked, touching my front wheel with his toe.

I studied the handlebars, found a smudge of something greasy, and rubbed at it with my thumb. It wouldn't come off, and I had to rub harder. "Not sure."

"Well, we all make it home sometime," he said, then started working on the shears again. Both of us seemed intent on our polishing – him on the shears, me on my handlebars.

Mac broke the silence. "One of Mr. Hartley's pictures is of her. Becca."

"Where?"

"Inside, on the wall," he said. "When she was pretty young."

Ask me to come in and see it. Ask me.

"Do you want to come in and see it?"

"Oh. Yeah, sure," I said, as if the idea hadn't occurred to me. I let my bike fall onto the grass and followed him into the entry. Immediately, Mr. Hartley appeared. He was dressed identically to the day before – same suspenders, same slippers. He had a folded newspaper under his arm.

"Hi, Mr. H," Mac said.

The old man squinted at me, then back to Mac. "I've told you before, young man. No unsupervised female visits. I believe I saw your sister leave a while ago."

My face was hot again. I wondered how many times Mac had snuck Alissa upstairs.

Mac didn't seem affected by Mr. Hartley. "I'm just showing her one of your pictures. Right here, in the stairway." He took the stairs two at a time, glancing at a few of the pictures, then stopped. "Here," he said, pointing at the dusty glass. "This is her."

I followed him, and Mr. Hartley trailed after us. When I got to Mac's step, he took one more up. The stairs were fairly narrow. Standing this close, I could smell Mac. It was a combination of sun on bare skin, and new grass, with an undertone of animals. A good animal smell, like puppies. I leaned toward the glass.

It was definitely Becca. She was a lot younger, closer to my age, or maybe a few years older. She was laughing, her mouth open, and a guy with long shaggy dark hair was brandishing a pair of plant clippers, pretending to cut the edge of her sleeve.

And her hair was red.

Long, and dark red. She looked like Alice in Wonderland, all girly and perfect. Except for the red hair.

"Her hair," I said, and realized I had my fingers on my own hair. Before I'd cut mine, it had been long, thickly hanging over my shoulders like Becca's.

"Who are you looking at?" Mr. Hartley asked. Mac and I each took one step up, so there was room for him.

"Ms. Jell," Mac said. "Becca, next door. That's her, isn't it? Except her hair's a different color."

Mr. Hartley pulled a pair of glasses out of his shirt pocket, and carefully fitted the wire arms over his ears, arranging them on the bridge of his nose. His mouth opened as he stared at the picture. "Oh. Oh, yes, that's Rebecca. That's her natural color. A real redhead. She was always coloring it, though. Yes, that's her, with Nigel."

Mac and I looked at each other.

"Who's Nigel?" I asked.

Mr. Hartley looked up at me. His eyes were magnified by his reading glasses, making him look like an alien. "My son," he answered. "He did the yard work for the Kjellbergs for a few years."

"The Kjellbergs?" I said.

"Yes," he replied, looking back to the picture and nodding. "Yes. Rebecca shortened her name for the stage. Becca. Yes. From Rebecca Kjellberg to Becca Jell."

I glanced up at Mac again. "And Nigel worked there? In the yard?"

"Yes. For a while, anyway. Until . . ."

We waited for him to continue, but he just kept looking at the picture. I couldn't stand it any longer.

"Until what, Mr. Hartley? What happened?"

Mr. Hartley took off his glasses, folded them, and eased them back into his pocket. He busied himself patting his pockets, fussing with the newspaper. "Harald – that was Rebecca's father – he didn't approve of Nigel. At least not of Nigel and Rebecca."

"They went out?"

"Harald wouldn't let Rebecca have a normal life, do the things young people do. But she'd sneak over here, and she and Nigel spent a lot of time together."

Mr. Hartley made a sad *hmmm*ing sound in his throat. "Eventually Nigel went off to Montreal, to McGill University, and Rebecca was starting to get little acting parts around the city." He stopped. "But she – Rebecca – always seemed younger than she was. There was something very . . ." he searched for the right word, "vulnerable about her. Something trusting." He sighed. "She always talked about leaving, about going to the States, where she hoped she'd be 'discovered.' That was her word for it. And then, one day Rebecca was gone.

Both Rebecca and Rakel. Left the old boy — Rebecca's father — alone."

I shifted my weight. It seemed like Mac stirred, too, ever so slightly, so that we each moved an inch closer to each other. I was probably imagining it. "So Becca and Rakel left. And what about Nigel? Did he try to find her?"

Mr. Hartley's face closed, his shoulders stiffening. "The relationship died a natural death." He leaned toward the picture again, sighing. "She'd meant a great deal to him. Young love." He shook his head. "He was a good boy, my Nigel. Still is. Loyal."

"Where did she go? Was that when she went to Hollywood?"

Mr. Hartley looked down at his newspaper, pinching the fold over and over. "I'm not entirely sure. She was gone for a long time. And while she was away, Harald destroyed all her rosebushes. Just cut them right down, and dug out the roots. Rebecca had loved those roses, Nigel told me. It must have been pure spite, old Kjellberg doing such a thing.

"When she eventually came back, I'd see her sitting in her yard, looking at the empty spaces where the roses had been. She was a changed girl, and she never seemed the same again. Something was gone; perhaps her sense of spirit. Maybe it was because she hadn't made the success of herself that she thought. It must have been difficult for her to come back here after living the life of an actress. But her asthma was getting worse then, too. Luckily Harald left her well provided for, financially."

"And they never saw each other again? Nigel and Becca?"

The old man's head shook back and forth, slowly and heavily. "Nigel didn't get home much after that. Studying hard, and the expense of travel." He started down the stairs. "Harald Kjellberg was a bitter old fool. First drove away his wife, and then his daughter. Died alone. That was a nasty bit of business."

"What was?"

"He died over one winter, but no one knew. He didn't have any friends. It wasn't until his mail started piling up outside that I suspected something was wrong. When this went on for a few weeks, I eventually called the police. They found his body."

"Gross," I said. That must have been what Dad remembered.

"And after that, Rebecca came home and stayed. Planted her roses again." He started down the steps, his shoulders drooping. At the bottom he looked back up at us. "No girls upstairs," he said again, but quietly, without the stern tone he'd used the first time.

I came down the steps. "I'm going, Mr. Hartley," I said. As I passed him, he reached out and touched my arm.

"I've met you before, haven't I?"

"You saw me yesterday," I said. "I was here, looking for Linnea and Tanner."

"Yes, I realize that, but it's something else." He kept looking into my face, then shrugged. "You have a familiar look." He took his newspaper from under his arm and walked back into his apartment, closing the door behind him.

I looked up at Mac, still standing near the picture of Becca. "I better go," I said. "But it's weird, eh? How she called you Nigel?" I didn't say what else I was thinking – that she had been in love with Nigel when she was younger, and now she was calling Mac Nigel and acting all goofy and lovestruck. It was definitely freaky.

"Yeah," Mac said, walking down the stairs and following me out through the front door. As I got on my bike, he unlocked his from the step. "I have to go out for some bread and stuff. Wait a sec, and I'll ride with you."

We started along the road, pedaling slowly. We didn't talk, but it felt comfortable now. He followed me right to the raspberry house.

"This is my place," I said, stopping.

Mac looked at the house. "Wild color," he said.

"It's even wilder inside. And I don't mean the paint," I said. "They're driving me insane."

"Whose family doesn't?" Mac said, then pushed away from the curb.

"Bye," I said.

"Yeah," Mac replied.

I turned to go into my yard, but Mac called something.

"So, if you're ever riding by Palmerston Avenue, I'll probably see you again."

"Okay," I yelled. *Okay.*

I sat on the porch for a while after Mac drove away. I was thinking, thinking about all kinds of stupid things, things like toys in Becca's house. Like hands.

And like red hair.

SIXTEEN

I wanted desperately to go back to Palmerston Avenue, but I couldn't think of an excuse. I spent a lot of time on the front step, reading, writing letters to my friends in Vancouver, wondering why Kieran never wrote, and pushing Sandeep up and down the street in his stroller about a thousand times. Three days went by. Four. Mac never rode by. I tried not to let images of him and Alissa come into my head.

There was something about Mac – the way he let Becca call him Nigel without correcting her, the look of his hands oiling those shears, and how I knew they'd be hard with callouses from the yard work, and yet soft and gentle handling the animals at World o' Pets. Imagining him reading *The Runaway Bunny* to Tanner. It was hard to stop thinking about him.

Just like I couldn't stop thinking about Becca. I watched *The Sorrow Club* at least three more times, and practiced some of Becca's lines in front of the mirror over my dresser.

"Please don't leave me alone," I said, a hand to my throat, the way Becca's character had. "When will you be coming back for me?" I tied a white scarf over my hair, stepping back from the mirror and squinting my eyes, so that I could see what I would look like if I had platinum hair. Then I moved closer to the mirror and tried it again.

"Please don't leave me alone." I watched my hand at my throat, the shape of my lips as I spoke. The mirror was old and splotchy. Amoeba-like shapes swam on its surface, making me look strange. Older. For just a second, I scared myself. I backed away again, pulling the scarf off my head. Then I got out a recent copy of *People* magazine I'd bought, looking through the pages for a new picture for my *M* Book. But I couldn't find one.

Instead, another face, another image of a tall, red-haired woman filled my head.

I had to go back.

🌳

"I'm going out for a while," I whispered to Calypso. She was lying on her side on her bed, Sandeep snuggled up with his back tight against her huge bulge. He was asleep.

"Okay," she mouthed, and wrapped her arm tighter around Sandeep, smiling sleepily, sweetly, sort of a Madonna and child picture.

As I turned to leave, she whispered, "Did you see the letter on the kitchen table? I forgot to give it to you yesterday."

I nodded. It was in a thin blue envelope, addressed to me. I saw my mother's familiar writing, and the unfamiliar stamps. She must have found out where I was from Jan. I had folded it in half and put it in my back pocket.

I slowed my bike as I drove by Linnea's, but didn't even glance at the house, just in case Mac, at that very instant, was looking out the little painted-shut window upstairs. I wouldn't want him to see me staring.

I went to Becca's front door and rang the brass doorbell. Nobody answered, but I could hear a muted droning from inside. I rang the bell again, and the drone stopped. There was the sound of footsteps, and then the door swung open.

"What do you want?" It was Rakel. She had on the same navy dress and black stockings and shoes. On the foyer carpet beside her, I could see the snaking hose of a vacuum, and behind her was a tall, dark wood grandfather clock. The polished brass pendulum swung back and forth inside the glass door.

"Could I please see Becca?" I asked.

"She rests today. She is not well." Rakel started to close the door.

"Wait," I said, pushing at it. "Will you tell her I came to see her?"

She shook her head, her mouth gathered like a drawstring purse.

"You won't tell her?"

"Miss Becca doesn't need you coming around here, stirring so much up. You don't have friends your own age? Leave Miss Becca alone. She doesn't need you here," she said again.

Stirring what up? Why should the old witch care if I came? It's none of her business. As she started to close the door again, I saw, over her shoulder, a flash of color, the swish of something silky and flowered. In that flicker I remembered what Dad had said about Becca hiding behind the hall curtain, watching the door.

"Becca?" I said, louder than was necessary, just before the heavy wooden door closed in my face. It did close, with a *whoosh* of artificially cooled air, but almost immediately opened again.

"I thought I heard your voice," Becca said, "but I wasn't sure." She coughed, a hacking cough, followed by a wheeze. She was wearing a silky robe covered with mauve and pink roses, tightly belted around her thin waist. Her feet were bare.

Rakel stood behind her, her mouth pulled even tighter.

"Let's sit out here, where it's quieter," Becca said, stepping onto the open veranda. "This is Rakel's day to clean."

"Miss Becca, you need your rest. Don't go outside; you know it makes it worse if you move too much."

But Becca ignored her, firmly closing the door. "We'll sit here," she said, motioning toward two worn wicker chairs, with faded but thick cushions on the seats and backs. I followed, stopping behind her as she unexpectedly stood still.

"Who is that?" she asked.

A man walked slowly out from the side of the house. His head was down, and he was scribbling something on a clipboard.

Becca's chin rose. "May I enquire as to your business in my yard?" she called.

The man looked up, then stopped in front of the veranda. He tucked his pen into the clip on the top of the board. "City of Winnipeg, Community Services Department. We're working in cooperation with the Coalition to Save the Elms, checking the trees in this area. We put a notice in your mailbox last week to inform you that our people would be on the property."

"I don't read anything but personal letters and fan mail. And why are you checking the trees?"

"For Dutch elm disease. We try to cover most areas of the city every summer. You've got a lot of old elms here. There are a few that don't look in great shape."

I heard the sharp, raspy intake of Becca's breath. "Do any of them have it? The disease?"

The man frowned and rubbed his eye with one knuckle. "This is a preliminary check. But I've marked any that look sick. Sometimes it's Dutch elm, sometimes it's just a bad year for the tree. The cankerworms can weaken them a lot. Another crew will come out and do the final check. And if any have the disease, we'll take whatever steps are necessary."

Becca put her hand on my arm. "Steps?" Her breathing was now a steady wheezing.

"If we find the disease, the tree has to come down. It's infectious, and spreads to other trees. So don't be alarmed if you see a crew here, sometime in the next few weeks. Then we'll let you know for sure." He turned and went toward the gate.

"The tree has to come down?" Becca repeated. Her fingers were gripping my arm uncomfortably.

He looked over his shoulder. "If it has Dutch elm, yes. You have a good day, now."

Becca let go of my arm and moved backwards, lowering herself onto the chair. Her skin had that clammy white look that she'd had when I'd first seen her on the street, and she was panting in short, hard breaths.

"Shouldn't you get your inhaler?" I asked, sitting beside her.

She nodded, getting up, and motioning for me to follow her.

As we went into the foyer, the monstrous roar of the ancient vacuum came from the living room. Becca hooked her arm through mine, and I walked with her, slowly, up the stairs. She stopped once, bending over and coughing.

There was a beautiful stained glass window, a tree with a full green top, and then long tendrils of roots running down from the trunk, at the turn of the stairs. The upstairs hall was long and narrow, with three closed doors on either side.

Becca opened one and dropped my arm. She went to her bed and sat on it, reaching for the inhaler on the bedside table. I saw *The Glass Menagerie*, by Tennessee Williams, lying open on the table. Becca took her two puffs, then leaned back, struggling to breathe normally.

The room overlooked the river, and had a double window, open. The slight breeze made the sparkling white curtain at the window dance, every so slightly, along the bottom. This room didn't feel air-conditioned, but wasn't hot. It was fresh smelling, filled with the cooling air that wafted in from the river.

Her room was tidy, the double bed neatly made and covered with a satiny pale peach spread. Ruffled matching pillows were piled in a heap at the headboard, which was also covered with the same pale peach. There was a row of mirrored closet doors and, near the window, a deep chair and ottoman upholstered in peach and sage green. There was a tall dresser and, to one side of it, a wonderful expansive dressing table with a three-sided mirror. On the top of the dressing table was a collection of fancy perfume bottles and a beautiful tortoiseshell brush, comb, and hand mirror. In front of the table was a small skirted chair. I could imagine Becca sitting there, brushing her hair.

Becca got up and flung open one of the closet doors, and a light went on in the closet. "Do you want to see my costumes? I was able to keep some of the things I wore in various plays."

"Sure." I went over and looked in at the row of clothes in clear zipped plastic bags.

"This is one of my favorites," she said, pulling out a sleeveless, deep green dress, the color of old moss, with a flouncy layered skirt of lighter shades of the same green. There was cream-colored satin piping along the edge of each flounce. She held the dress up in front of her, then put it against me.

"Try it on," she said.

"No. It's okay."

"Here. Just slip it on over what you're wearing. You'll look fabulous in it."

She put it over my head, and I was forced to put my arms in the air as she slid it down. She zipped it up at the back, then stood behind me.

"Just look at that," she breathed. "It fits perfectly. It was actually made for me, specifically to my measurements. But it looks like it was made for you, too."

It did fit perfectly. Not too small, like my mother's clothes had been for the last two years; not too big, like Calypso's. I thought of "Goldilocks and the Three Bears." *This one is just right.* "I like it," I said, suddenly feeling shy as I gazed at my image in the mirrored door, surprised by how grown-up I looked in the elegant formal dress. It even made my body look different, the waist of the dress pulled in tightly and then curving out over the hips.

Becca was still looking over my shoulder, our faces reflected in the mirror side by side. We were exactly the same height.

"You have good bone structure. You must photograph well," she said.

I struck a pose, sucking in my cheeks and lowering my chin.

Becca suddenly left me, going to sit in front of her dressing table. She picked up one of her perfume bottles, absently running her fingers over its glass edges. I saw her raise her eyes, looking at me in the mirror.

I reached behind, struggling with the zipper of the dress, and finally got it undone, then slid the dress off. I hung it on the padded hanger, pulling the protective plastic back around it.

"Are you a Taurus?" she suddenly asked.

I turned around, staring at her. "Yes. May 5TH."

Her breath pulled in, one long wheezy gasp.

"How did you know?" I asked.

She didn't answer for a few seconds. "Oh, it's just that Taurus people are known to be passionate and demanding, with a strong creative drive. Lots of drama."

"My mother always called me a drama queen."

Becca stood, taking her inhaler from the bedside table. "No, my dear," she said, starting out the door. "*I'm* the drama queen around here."

I followed her down the stairs, and in the living room I breathed deeply and easily, feeling the cool calmness of the house as it washed over me. I looked at one of the rows of books in a tall polished-wood bookcase. As I read the titles and authors' names on the spines of the books, I realized that they were in order. Alphabetical order, by the author's last name. I thought of my own books and CD's, lined up neatly on the shelves in my bedroom.

There was a vase of flowers from Becca's garden — tall spiky purple delphiniums and something else, pink and soft, as well as lots of greenery — on the piano. I fingered the petals of the pink flowers.

"Aren't they pretty?" she asked.

"I love your whole house, Becca. It's so . . . perfect."

Becca laughed her high tinkly laugh. "It's hardly perfect, although I do love it. It feels empty, though. It's far too big for only two people. It's a house that should be filled, filled with voices and music, with children and pets. With a family gathered around the dining room table. With life." She sighed, sitting at the piano bench.

"It doesn't feel empty to me. It feels spacious. Quiet. A person can think here," I said, sitting on the chintz sofa. I heard a papery crinkle, and remembered the letter from Greece in my back pocket. I ran my fingers over the fabric of the couch, and saw that the basket of stuffed animals had been moved, and was now beside the piano bench.

"Becca? Whose toys are those?"

Becca looked down, then picked up a wooly monkey and ran her fingers over it. "You'll think I'm foolish," she said.

"No, I won't." She was probably going to tell me they were hers. The grandfather clock chimed softly. I counted. One. Two. Three. Still Becca didn't say anything. "I won't think you're foolish," I said. "Really."

Becca put her mouth onto the top of the monkey's head. "I buy them for my daughter," she said, her voice muffled by the monkey.

I looked at the monkey, and a shudder ran through me as I stared at its black, lifeless eyes. "Your daughter?"

Becca put the monkey on the bench and got up. She went to the patio door and stared out at her yard of flowers and trees, and at the river beyond. "Each year." Her voice was clear, even though she had her back to me. "I gave her one when she was born. And I buy one every year."

I became aware that the vacuum had stopped. I couldn't move.

Suddenly Becca turned and looked at me. There were tears on her cheeks.

"Your daughter?" I said again, aware of how high my voice had become.

She wiped her cheeks with the palms of her hands, then held her hands out to me. They were empty, but the way she cupped them together made me feel as if there were something there, something invisible, something she was offering me, if I could only see it. Then she crossed the room and opened the door of one of the glassed bookshelves. She took out a box with a small lock on it. The box was square, and about the size of a chocolate box, made of a shiny, creamy substance that looked like shell.

"Is that mother-of-pearl?" I asked.

She nodded, setting the box on the top of the bookshelf. Then she put her hand up and touched the tiny key that hung beside the leaf on the necklace I'd never seen her without. She caressed the key between her fingers.

"I don't know if this is the right time." She was still rubbing the key between her fingers. "Upstairs, just now, I . . . no. It's too soon."

At that moment Rakel came into the room, a rag in her hand, and began to dust the piano as if we weren't there. Or at least as if I weren't there.

Becca quickly put the box back into the bookshelf and closed the glass door.

"Oh, Miss Becca, you should have your slippers on. This is not good," Rakel said, frowning at me as if I had personally taken away Becca's slippers. She came up to her, tucking a piece of Becca's hair behind one ear, smoothing it with her gnarled old hand. "Shall I pour your tea, Miss Becca?" she asked. "I have it all ready for you in the kitchen. And your favorite biscuits. Did you take your Ventolin? The girl must go now, and you can have your tea." She glared at me. "Tea is always at three o'clock."

"Not yet," Becca said. "I was just going to show Poppy some of my signed photos. From Hollywood."

Why is she lying to Rakel? She had been about to show me what was in the box. I glanced at it. I wanted to stay. "I saw *The Sorrow Club*," I said. "Linnea — Mac's sister — lent it to me. You were great."

Becca picked up the monkey and put it back into the basket with the other animals. "I was offered different roles after that, but nothing felt right. I wasn't one of those actresses who will take anything that comes along. I have standards."

I didn't mention that I'd heard about the commercials.

"That's why I preferred the stage," Becca went on. "There are more opportunities."

"Miss Becca," Rakel interrupted. "Your tea."

Becca was lightly running her fingers over the keyboard now, not pressing hard enough to make a sound. But she was humming.

"So. I will see you out," Rakel said.

"There's no need. I know the way," I said, trying to make my voice match Rakel's snobby tone. "Good-bye, Becca," I said, raising my voice, moving toward the foyer.

She still didn't look up from the keys. "Poppy?" Her breathing was growing raspier again.

I stopped. "Yes?"

"You will come back, won't you? Tell me you'll come back." She looked up finally, her face troubled.

The same shivery feeling I'd had earlier, when Becca had said "I buy them for my daughter," returned.

Before I could answer, Becca's fingers pressed down, and a loud chord sounded, making me jump. Rakel hurried toward me, giving a slight push on my shoulder. "Go. Go now."

"But —" I said, trying to look over her shoulder at Becca, but the old lady was blocking my view. "I'll come another time," I called, as Rakel half pushed me into the foyer.

"No," Rakel whispered, her face close to mine. I smelled raw onions and false teeth. "Don't come again. You upset her." She opened the front door, still walking so close to me that I was forced to step outside. "Don't come again. Do you hear me?" she said, and closed the door, softly but firmly, right in my face.

SEVENTEEN

I stared at myself in the bathroom mirror. I held up my hands and looked at them, then leaned closer to the mirror, looking, searching my reflection. "It looks like it was made for you," I said out loud, remembering what Becca had said about the dress I'd tried on. *It's in the locked box. What I need to see is in the locked box.*

"Who are you talking to?" Dad called through the closed door. "You gonna be long?" I heard the rustle of newspaper. "I need in there before supper."

I cleared my throat. "Nobody. And I'm coming out." I opened the door.

"What's up?" Dad asked. "You look like you've seen a ghost."

I just brushed by him, going down to the kitchen.

Calypso was cooking rice and some other strange-smelling concoction at the stove. "There were a few things for you in the mail today," she said. "And a note. They're all there, on the table."

There were two envelopes and a folded piece of paper. By the return address, I saw that one letter was from my friend Danielle. I would read it in my room later. The other one was another blue airmail envelope. Already. One yesterday, and one today.

"How's your mother doing?" Calypso asked.

"I wouldn't know," I said, sitting at the table beside Sandeep. He was scribbling on the back of an envelope with a yellow crayon. I opened the folded paper.

"But what does she say? In her letters?"

"I don't read them," I said. "I don't care what she has to say."

"I don't care," Sandeep said. "Jimmy Cack Corn, and I don't care."

"Hi, Poppy," the note said. The writing was dark and firm. "I stopped by, but you weren't home. Do you want a kitten? Come by World o' Pets if you do. I work all day tomorrow. Mac."

I looked at Calypso, whistling as she stirred and clanked lids off and on the pots at the stove. "Did you talk to him?"

"Who?" Calypso asked, dumping squares of tofu into the rice.

"Mac. The note's from him."

"Oh, yeah." She turned from the rice. "He has a beautiful smile, doesn't he?"

I nodded.

"I'm glad you're meeting some people your own age," Calypso said. She suddenly reached out and gripped the back of one of the kitchen chairs.

"What's wrong?" I asked. There was a deep line between Calypso's eyebrows.

"I'm sure it's nothing. I just went weak for a minute." She let go of the chair. "Isn't that nice, Eric?" she asked Dad, as he came into the kitchen. "Poppy has a friend. Linnea's brother, Mac."

Dad walked by and tapped me on the top of the head with his newspaper. "Could this be the beginning of a romance?" he asked.

I pushed away from the table, my chair scraping across the floor with a loud and angry sound. "Of course not. He's not my type. And besides, he's got a girlfriend. Not only that, but I have a boyfriend at home." I waved Danielle's letter. "This is from him. So I'm not interested in any *romance*, Dad."

"You have a boyfriend? You never mentioned him," Calypso said.

"Maybe I don't tell everyone my complete life history," I said. "Can we get another cat?"

"Sure," Calypso said, just as Dad said, "No."

I looked at them as they looked at each other.

"Why not?" Calypso asked.

"Three is enough," Dad answered.

"There's always room for one more," Calypso said.

"Of some things," Dad said, winking at me. "But not cats."

The next morning I looked up World o' Pets in the phone book, then rode down Portage Avenue looking for it. It wasn't that far. I'd had a horrible sleep. I kept thinking about Becca, and the look on her face when she came toward me, her empty hands seeming full of something I couldn't see. Her face was soft and, in a way, more beautiful than it had ever looked. It was like she was, for that moment, totally at peace.

"Hi," I said, when I went in. Mac was there, weighing a shih tzu puppy.

"Oh, hi. You got my note?" He cuddled the puppy against his chest.

"Yeah. How adorable," I said, rubbing my fingers on the dog's soft curly head.

"Here. You can hold this one. I've got a few more to weigh," he said, and put the little thing in my arms. It wriggled and licked my face.

"I haven't seen you around," I finally said, trying for casual.

"I had to go home. An emergency, sort of." He mumbled the last few words.

"Home?"

"Mac!" someone called. We both turned.

It was Alissa, behind the counter. She was wearing the same dumb safari outfit as Mac. "Did we get a new supply of heartworm pills?"

"Yeah. They came in yesterday."

"Thanks."

"She works here?" I asked, looking at Alissa.

"Yeah. Her boyfriend works here, too. He was in a couple of my classes at school. He actually got me the job."

"Her boyfriend?" I tried not to let the words explode out of my mouth in a joyous rush.

"Yeah. Why?"

I was glad he was busy with the puppies. "Nothing. So she's still going out with him?"

Now Mac looked at me. "Yeah."

"It's just that – when I saw you at the street festival – I just thought that you and her . . . you know. . . ."

"Me and Alissa? Uh-uh. She's not my type," he said.

There was a comfortable silence as I stroked the puppy. "So you said there was a problem? At home?"

He nodded, not looking at me. "Just some stuff to clear up."

The puppy settled down, and I rubbed my nose against the top of its soft little head. "Do you miss your parents? Not living with them?"

Mac's mouth twisted strangely, and I saw a flash of dark brown in his eyes. "Nah," he said. "They're pretty messed up. You're lucky, you know," he said, taking a puppy off the scale.

"Me? Why?"

"Because your mother's out doing something with her life."

"What's so neat about my mother doing something weird like going off to Greece?"

Mac rubbed the puppy's silky ear between his fingers. "Because she's not playing it safe and predictable. She's taking a chance, and that says that there's something brave about her. If you saw my parents . . . they live in a small town, and probably not all small towns are like this, but in mine, people are supposed to follow certain paths. And for people who don't follow those paths . . . well, they can get treated pretty bad." I suddenly wondered if my own mind was the small town type.

"My parents wouldn't help Linnea when she got pregnant, and she had nowhere to turn. But she came here to Winnipeg, and made it on her own." He cleared his throat. "So, do you want the kitten?" he asked, putting his puppy and mine back with their brothers and sisters. "She's the last one of a litter," he said. "And she's really past the best-selling stage. My boss asked me if I knew anyone who'd want her."

We walked to the wire cage with the carpet-wrapped post in the center. A white kitten was curled into a ball in one corner. She looked so alone, her back pressed against the wire.

"She's so sweet," I said. "Why didn't anyone buy her?"

Mac opened the cage and took her out. She hung stiffly in his hand, her legs tensed. "Who knows? It just happens. And we're pretty sure she's deaf, so when we tell people that, it turns them off." He handed her to me, and she immediately relaxed against my chest.

"Deaf?"

"She's got two different colored eyes. That can be a sign, and she doesn't respond to noise."

I rubbed under the kitten's chin, and she purred, her front claws opening and closing on my bare arm, but so gently that it didn't hurt. One of her eyes was green, and the other blue.

"You don't want her?" I asked Mac.

"I would, but Mr. Hartley's got this strict no-pets policy. I just thought of your place, with your little brother and all."

"We already have three, and my dad says no more."

Mac reached for the kitten, but she resisted, pushing harder into me. She seemed to need somebody to love her.

"What will happen if no one buys her?"

Mac didn't look at me, concentrating on scratching behind the kitten's ears. "We have to give her to the Humane Society."

"But if no one takes her from there . . ."

"Yeah. They only keep them a month."

"And then?"

Mac finally looked at me. His eyes were flat brown. "What do you think?" He fussed with the latch of the cage. "They have to put her down."

"Mac," I said. It felt good to say his name out loud.

He left the latch and stroked the kitten's back. "What?"

"What about Becca?" I thought of her empty hands again. "Maybe she would like the kitten. For company."

Mac rubbed his hand down the kitten's back once more. His fingers touched my arm. "Maybe," he said. "She might act a little nuts sometimes, but I think she's okay underneath it all."

"I think so, too," I said. *And there's more underneath it all. And I have to find out what it is. If what I'm thinking can possibly be true.*

I looked through the bushes of Mac's yard. I didn't want to chance running into Rakel if I came through Becca's front yard. Becca was there, under her tree. She was wearing the dress I'd first seen her wearing when I'd met her on Palmerston Avenue.

"Becca," I called, in a loud whisper. "Becca. Over here."

Becca's head turned quickly, toward the bushes. "Is that you, Poppy?" she said, breathlessly. I didn't know if it was her asthma or excitement.

"Yeah," I said. "Is it safe for me to come in the yard?"

Becca pushed her hair away from her face. "Of

course. Why not?" She beamed at me. "I'm so glad you're here. Come. Come and sit with me."

I pushed through the bushes, holding the cardboard carrier with the holes in it in front of me. I saw a red plastic ribbon tied around the tree, and thought of the man with the clipboard yesterday. Becca's tree was marked. It might have Dutch elm disease.

"I have something for you," I said, sitting on the grass under the tree with her, the box on my lap. Inside, the kitten was still.

Becca clapped her hands together and grinned like Sandeep does when I make funny faces at him. "What is it?"

I put the box in her lap. "Open it."

Becca unfolded the flaps of the peaked top and looked inside. She exhaled – one long, slow breath. "This is for me?"

"I didn't know if you liked cats. Or if Rakel – or if you would want it. It's a girl."

She lifted it out and, just as it had done with me, the kitten immediately settled against Becca, pushing her nose against Becca's arm. "She's beautiful. Oh, so sweet," she said, putting her face down against the kitten's back.

"I know. And no one wanted her. She might be deaf," I said. "Is that okay?"

Becca raised her head. "I don't care. Poor thing. All alone, with no one to love her."

"So you'll keep her?"

"Of course! Of course. I love her already. And I know what I'll name her. Blanche, because she had nowhere to go and had to depend on the kindness of strangers," she said. "Do you know the play *A Streetcar Named Desire*, Poppy?"

I looked down at my feet, stretched out in front of me. "Yes," I said, wanting to say, "Don't you remember? Don't you remember how we met?" But I didn't. "And *blanche* is French for white. So it's a perfect name," I said.

"It was in New Orleans that I played Blanche DuBois onstage," Becca went on. "Or was it in Chicago? No. I played Madame Ranevsky in Chicago, in *The Cherry Orchard*." She stroked the kitten in a distracted way, staring up at the branches of the tree.

The kitten stayed curled in her lap, purring. Becca looked down at it. She smiled at the kitten, and then up at me. "I've never had a pet," she said.

"Never?"

"No. My father wouldn't allow it. He said animals could carry vermin." She sighed. "He worried too much. He was far too overprotective. Always sure that something terrible would befall me." She kept on stroking the kitten. "And then, after – after I left – we traveled around too much. Rakel and I. It would have been too difficult to have any . . ." she paused ". . . attachments. I couldn't have any. If you're going to devote yourself to a career like acting, you shouldn't have any attachments."

What an odd word to use.

"My little baby," Becca murmured, picking up the kitten and kissing its nose. "Sweet little baby. Mommy will get you some warm milk in a minute." She set the kitten back in her lap, then looked straight into my face. "I had a baby," she said. "A sweet little baby girl. I told you that, yesterday."

I swallowed.

"Yes," Becca said. "I couldn't keep her. Rakel and I agreed. And she was so beautiful, with her red hair." She reached out and touched my hair, the same look on her face as I'd seen yesterday, when she studied my face in her bedroom mirror.

Oh my God. Oh my God.

"Oh, good," she said, looking into the box. "You brought some food. Is this the best kind for a kitten?" she asked, putting her hand back onto Blanche's head.

I couldn't concentrate. I couldn't think about anything but what it seemed was staring me in the face.

"It's strange," Becca went on, not seeming to notice that I didn't answer her. She turned to look behind her, at the tree and its red ribbon. "I was feeling so terrible about my tree today, imagining how I'd feel if it had to die. And now you've brought me this new and lovely little friend."

I just sat there, and Becca went on. "What's strange is the way things work together. Sometimes when you lose something you love and the pain is almost unbearable, something else comes into your life to fill the emptiness."

"I have to go now," I said, getting up. My voice sounded fuzzy in my ears, as if I were underwater. "I have to go."

"Already? But you've only just come, and there's so much for us to talk about."

I pushed through the bushes.

"Thank you," she called. "For Blanche, and for everything. Come back soon. Soon, Poppy."

🌳

I couldn't go back to the raspberry house. Not yet. I rode my bike around for the next little while, up and down streets, not looking at anything, just thinking, putting little pieces together. Finally I stopped at Vimy Ridge Park and sat on a bench.

It can't be.

But I couldn't stop thinking about it.

I worked and rearranged the pieces, turning over each fact, examining it to see how it would fit in place, the way Calypso had with her old quilt blocks.

Is it all part of some weird fate thing? How can there be so many coincidences? I thought of what I had said to Calypso, about meeting my mother on the street. I thought about this weird pull that drew me back to Palmerston Avenue. About all the ways Becca and I were alike, not only physically, but in other ways.

About Nigel. Becca would have had her baby at the Misericordia.

Even Mr. Hartley had a moment of thinking I looked familiar. *Does he recognize something in me? Some similarity to Becca when she was young?*

My head ached with a strange rocking sensation, like I'd been spinning in circles. I closed my eyes, trying to stop the rocking, but all I could see was Becca's face, and the way she'd looked at me when she touched my hair, the eager look on her face when she saw me today.

She knows, too, by my birthday, by my hair, my shape, by everything.

She knows, too, and she must be feeling overwhelmed, like I am.

She knows, too.

EIGHTEEN

I rode my bike around the streets aimlessly. I couldn't face the raspberry house and Calypso and Sandeep, not the way I was feeling. I had a strange gnawing in my stomach, and bought a Peanut Buster parfait at Dairy Queen, but after two spoonfuls it made my stomach feel even more strange, and I realized I wasn't hungry at all. In fact, I felt like I needed to throw up. I really just wanted to sneak up to my room, lie on my bed, and think about everything. But as I got close to the raspberry house, I saw the Karpet King van parked in front.

Just my luck, Dad coming home in the middle of the afternoon. One more roadblock to prevent me from having some quiet time to think.

I left my bike on the grass in the front yard, and then went and sat in the truck, wishing I had the keys, so I could at least turn on the radio. I noticed a wrinkled Caramilk wrapper on the dashboard.

"Poppy?"

I jumped.

Dad stuck his face in the open window. "What are you doing, sitting in here?"

I didn't answer him. "Why are *you* home?"

"Calypso called me. She isn't feeling well. Just after lunch she fainted. Luckily Sandeep was asleep, and Calypso didn't hurt herself. We've had the midwife in, and she said Calypso's blood pressure is high and she's got edema. A lot of water retention. It's not too serious yet, and often happens later in pregnancy, but to be safe Calypso should stay in bed for a few days at least. Keep off her feet and take things easy." Dad slid his eyes toward me. "So it's a good thing you're here. I can't afford to take any time off work — not that they'd give me any. In fact, I had signed up for extra evening hours to make some overtime. Can we count on you, Poppy, to stay home and take care of Sandeep until Calypso's blood pressure is down? If it doesn't lower, the midwife said, Calypso could have to go to the hospital. And you know how hard that would be on her, Poppy. She's so nervous about hospitals."

"Dad," I said. "I've got a lot of things going on in my life right now. Important things that you have no clue about. I have to be able to come and go." I had to go back to Palmerston. I needed to tell Becca I knew, and find out what we would do about it.

I imagined what it would be like to live in the house on Palmerston. The beautiful quiet house, with soft colors and organized bookshelves and delicate glasses and Becca playing classical music on the piano. I wouldn't think about my life in Vancouver right now. My friends, and the ocean and mountains. Mom, and what her face would look like when I told her.

"She trusts you completely with Sandeep," Dad said. "She's always telling me how glad she is you're here now to help us out." He rubbed his hand over his eyes. "I don't know what to do, Poppy."

Neither do I, Dad. Neither do I.

But he kept rubbing his eyes, and finally walked away, leaving me sitting in the van, staring at the Caramilk wrapper.

It took three days in bed before Calypso was able to get back into her routine, but she still had to be careful, up for half an hour, lying down for an hour.

I'd pretty much done everything around the house the first day, and into the evening while Dad worked, but on the second evening, when Dad got home a bit earlier, before it was dark, I rode over to Palmerston and rang Becca's bell.

I rang it a second time, and a third, but no one came. From inside, I heard the muted chiming of the grandfather clock in the foyer, and counted the eight softly echoing bongs.

I went over again on the third evening, and this time, almost as soon as I'd pressed the doorbell, the door opened. It was Rakel. I waited for her to tell me to get lost when I asked if I could see Becca. But she didn't, at least not in so many words.

"Miss Becca sleeps now," she said, her voice low. "Her health is worse. She can have no visitors."

She wasn't wearing her navy dress, but a long, frumpy patterned skirt and white blouse. On her feet were flat brown leather sandals, and without her hard black shoes she wasn't as tall as she had been before. She looked smaller, and ordinary, like someone's grandmother. Her eyes were shaded with weariness. And something else.

"Will she . . . will Becca be . . . all right?" I asked.

"It is a bad spell," Rakel said, her tone expressionless. "Some times are worse than others. She must rest for a number of days, with no disturbances." I knew that she was telling me not to come back.

"Could you tell her that I came to see her? I really want to talk to her."

"I will tell her," Rakel said, and then shut the door.

Wheeling my bike out of the yard, I looked at Mac's place, then took a deep breath and, leaving my bike beside the step, went in. I expected Mr. Hartley to pounce on me as I tiptoed up the stairs, but he didn't make an appearance.

I knocked on Linnea's door, and she opened it.

"I was just riding by, and thought that maybe Mac would be home," I said.

"Sorry. He's not," she said. "But I think he was trying to phone you earlier."

"Really?" I said, as if it were no big deal.

"He's out somewhere, now," she said. "Sorry."

"That's okay. It doesn't matter. Don't even bother to tell him I came by," I said, talking too fast. "It was nothing important," I added, knowing, as I did, that I was overdoing it.

I clattered down the stairs and rode home, fast. It *was* something important. I wanted to tell him about Becca. I knew he would understand. I had to talk to someone about the whole thing – Becca and me – or my head would burst open.

As I got in the door, Dad held the phone out. "For you."

I looked at it. "It's not Mom, is it? Because I don't want to talk to her." *Who else would phone me?*

"Actually, she did call. Just a few minutes ago. But this isn't her."

It was Mac. "Linnea said you came by. We must have just missed each other."

"Yeah. I went to see Becca. But she was sick, so I thought, I don't know. . . ." I waited for him to say something, but he didn't. "So, do you want to come over?"

"Sure," he said, without even a second's hesitation.

He was on the front porch in about ten minutes. "Let's stay out here," I said. There was no place to hang out inside. Dad was in the living room fiddling with his guitar, playing little riffs, and Calypso was sitting at the kitchen table cutting out quilt pieces. Even though Sandeep should have been asleep, I could hear him upstairs, singing and running around.

We sat on the step.

"Can I tell you something? Something so incredible?" I said. I couldn't be bothered to waste time talking about small, unimportant things. This was too huge. And so I told him, in the way that made it sound the most logical, about Becca. About the daughter she given up for adoption. About how I'd been adopted from the Misericordia Hospital. About all the things Becca had said and done – how she'd almost come right out and told me that I was her . . . the daughter she had to give away.

Mac shook his head. "Oh, man," he said. "That's pretty heavy. Are you sure?"

"Yeah. I'm sure. Every single little piece fits. I even know where she keeps the stuff about . . . about me. She showed it to me – the box."

"Have you seen it? Whatever stuff she has?"

"No. But I will. The next time I see her."

He was quiet for a few minutes, looking out at the street. I watched the side of his face. I could see a faint line of soft stubble on his jawline. I wanted to touch it. I heard Dad singing softly, a song I'd heard on one of his records. "Honey Bee."

"Poppy?" Mac turned to me. "I don't get it."

"What? That she could be my real mom?"

"No. Why you'd want her to be."

I blinked. "What do you mean?"

"She's so eccentric. Sickly, and strange. She has a weird life, all alone with the old lady." We heard Sandeep laughing through an upstairs bedroom window, and Calypso's voice, murmuring. "I mean, you're already so lucky."

Again with the lucky.

"You've got the mother who's in Greece. She sounds pretty cool to me. And you've got your dad, and Calypso, who's technically your stepmother. They treat you right, don't they?"

I put my chin on my palm, and rested my elbow on my knee. "Yeah. So?"

"So why are you so excited to dig up another mother? You've got two already. Most people are lucky to have one, and even then it can be a bust."

"But Mac," I said. "I'm talking about my *real* mother, not an adopted one or a stepmother. I'm talking about the connection of blood. The way that connection is so special, so huge that it can make you finally feel that you know who you are."

"Does anyone ever really know who they are?"

"Of course," I said. "You must know that feeling. You have your real parents. You don't have an empty place inside, waiting to be filled."

The living room behind us was silent now, no sound from Dad or his guitar.

Mac didn't say anything for a while, just looked away, and back to the darkening street. The streetlights flickered and then came on, throwing long shadows over the cars and road and sidewalk. It got darker on the step, and everything slowed down. I could hear the soft in and out of Mac's breathing. If I moved my left leg half an inch, I would connect with his right leg.

I knew something was going to happen.

"What island is your mother on?" he asked, still facing the street.

"Crete," I said.

"When you talk to her, or write to her, will you ask her about Knossos?" he said. "It's an ancient ruined city on Crete. There's a myth about Minotaur there, a half-man, half-bull monster. I'd love to find out, firsthand, what the ruins are like."

His leg was against mine now.

I wanted to tell him that I didn't talk to my mother, or write to her. I wanted to tell him that I used to like someone named Kieran Wasylik, but I could barely remember what he looked like now, and it didn't matter anyway because my friend Danielle had written to tell me that he was going out with some stuck-up snob named Vanessa, who lived in Point Grey.

I wanted him to tell me that it was the most wonderful thing in the world that I had found my real mother, and that my real home, the one I truly belonged in, was the big, beautiful, clean house on Palmerston Avenue.

"So you think the empty place is there because you don't know your birth mother," he said.

"Yes." I wanted him to turn toward me.

"And you think that Becca can make you feel complete?"

"Yes."

"And what if you get to know her really well, and she doesn't? What if —" A car drove by, its tires making a tiny *click-click* on the smooth pavement of the street, and we both watched it. Then Mac continued. "What if it's you who has to fill it? I mean, should we depend on someone else to finish us? To make us who we are?"

I didn't want him to say this. It wasn't what I wanted to hear. I wanted him to celebrate with me. To tell me that it was great, that everything would be perfect now. And I wanted him to turn his head, because then he would see, on my face, what I really wanted him to do next.

I knew he would. The feeling was too strong, sitting there in the fragrant darkness, crickets gently singing a sad little song, our legs touching.

But in the next instant the porch light flashed on, flooding us in brilliant light. We both jumped up, although I'm not sure why.

"What are you kids doing out here?" Dad said, through the screen door. He was wearing a pair of baggy sweatpants and no shirt. His hair was messy, sticking up in strange places. Even his mustache was rumpled. He squinted at us – a skinny, hairy Mr. Magoo. "I finally got Sandeep to sleep. Had to rock him for the last half an hour. You want anything to eat? Some juice?"

"No," I said. The crickets were silent.

"Well, I better split," Mac said. "See you, okay?"

"Sure. See you," I answered. "And I'll ask my mother about Knossos, if I remember," I called after him.

"Have you been writing to your mother?" Dad said, holding the door open for me. "I just heard you say –"

"No." *Why did he have to come to the door, at that very moment? Why couldn't he just leave me alone?* "I was just making conversation. I'm not going to write to her. And I told you I'm not going to talk to her if she phones."

"You should. She wants so badly to hear from you, Poppy. It's not fair to just abandon her."

"Me? Abandon her? That's funny," I said, and tried to laugh, but only a strangled snort came out. "And nothing is fair, anyway. Nothing." That same weird sound came out. I hated it. It sounded almost like a sob.

Dad put his arm around my shoulder and said, "It's late, Teddy Bear. Things will look better in the morning," and I let myself relax against him, for just a second, before I pulled away. But in that second I remembered – a kind of faded volume-turned-down memory – him and Mom calling me Teddy Bear a long, long time ago.

Round and round the garden, Dad's fingers went, in small circles, on my inner arm, *like a teddy bear.*

One step, two steps – his fingers walked up the inside of my arm,

Tickle you under there! and he tickled me under the arm.

"Again, Daddy," I'd laughed. "Do it again."

And he always did.

NINETEEN

Remembering how Dad had played that game with me when I was little made me think that maybe I could trust him with this. With this huge, amazing fact that Becca Jell was my mother.

I felt jumpy all day, writing a few letters, watching *The Sorrow Club* one more time, even playing some of Dad's records to kill time. Maybe it was because all I'd heard for so long – since I'd got here – was blues, or maybe it was just the way I was feeling, but I started to get into the music. There really was a catchy rhythm to it. And almost every song was about how someone wanted someone or something they couldn't have, or that they had lost.

Dad came home early, and we ate early. As soon as we were done supper, Dad went out to the backyard to fix a broken board in the fence. I followed him, and, standing behind him as he hammered, told him about Becca.

He looked over his shoulder and laughed. Laughed. "Good Lord, Poppy," he said, taking a nail out of his mouth. "That woman who's the washed-up actress?"

"Don't call her that! And it's true. I have all the evidence."

"When I see it, this evidence, then I'll believe it," he said, and laughed again, shaking his head and turning back to hammer the nail into the splintered wood.

I turned and ran into the house, up to my room, and threw myself on my bed. "I hate you," I said. "I hate you." I don't know what I had expected, but it wasn't laughter.

🌳

"Sandee! Sandee, come here, son." Dad's voice sounded as if he were calling through a cardboard tube.

I tried to open my eyelids, but they were so heavy.

"Poppy sleeping," Sandeep said, right into my face.

"Yeah. I was sleeping," I said, pushing back the quilt. It was almost dark. I turned on the lamp beside my bed, having to close my eyes against the sudden glare. I opened one eye enough to glance at my watch. Nine o'clock. I'd been sleeping for a couple of hours.

"Sandee go potty," Sandeep whispered.

I sat up. "Where? Did you go in my room?" I asked, scanning the floor for evidence.

Dad stopped in the open doorway, holding Sandeep's potty. "Success!" he beamed, carefully waving the pot. "He did it in the pot. Good boy, Sandee," he said, like Sandeep was a puppy that finally figured out what the newspaper was for. "Wait until Calypso gets home from her walk. She'll be one happy lady."

"Dad, please. Go and dump it."

"I'm on my way. Wait until Calypso hears about this," he repeated, smiling fondly at Sandeep. "You did it for your old dad, didn't you, Sandee?" Then he looked back at me. "Are you sick? Your eyes look sore. Hope you're not coming down with anything," he said cheerfully, and then left, carefully balancing the pot. It was as if I'd never even told him about Becca and me.

"I'm not sick," I said, even though he was gone. *How could a man get to be so old and not realize what it looks like when someone's been crying?*

"Sad Poppy," Sandeep said, climbing onto my bed. He gently rubbed one of Didi's corners against my left eye. For some reason it made me want to cry again, him such a little guy, and figuring out more than my own father.

"Yeah. I'm sad," I said. I heard the toilet flushing.

"Why?"

I shrugged, and put my arms around him. "I'm just sad, that's all, Sandeep."

He rested his cheek against mine. "Poor Poppy," he said, and then turned himself around so that we were spoons, his back curved against my front the way I'd seen him sleeping with Calypso.

Holding his warm little body, I felt some of the worry draining out of me, and I closed my eyes, snuggling tighter against Sandeep. I recognized the contented sound of him sucking his thumb.

I let myself drift close to sleep again, then heard a sigh.

Calypso was leaning against my door frame. "I wish I had a camera," she whispered. "I think he's asleep."

At her voice, Sandeep stirred. "No. No sleep. Sandee go potty," he mumbled.

Calypso must have had the same faith in Sandeep that I did. Her eyes darted to the floor. "Where?" she asked.

"In potty. Go potty in potty," Sandeep said. "Poppy sad."

I expected Calypso to jump up and down about Sandeep's news, but instead she said, "Poppy's sad?" then came in and sat beside me, putting her hand on Sandeep's curly head.

I felt my eyes sting again.

Dad came in. "Did you hear the good news, Calypso? Did Sandeep tell you what he did?"

"Take him out, would you, Eric?" Calypso said. "I'm staying here for a few minutes." She gently pulled Sandeep away from me, mouthing "bed" to Dad.

He nodded, lifting Sandeep, who clung to him limply. "We should celebrate, later," he said.

Calypso and I both looked at him.

"About the potty," he added. But when neither of us said anything, he said, "Alrighty, then," and left. I saw, over Dad's shoulder, that Sandeep's eyes were closed again.

Calypso wasn't looking at me, but down, at the crumpled quilt. "Did something happen?" she asked.

"Dad didn't tell you? He didn't tell you what I told him?"

She shook her head. "We really haven't had a quiet minute to talk since supper," she said.

I'd told Mac, and all he did was ask a bunch of questions I didn't have answers to. I'd told Dad, and he'd laughed at me. How could it be any worse? I might as well tell Calypso.

"Are you missing your mom?" she asked, running her hand over the pattern of the quilt.

"No."

"You know that she phoned last night, don't you?"

I nodded my head.

"She needs to talk to you, Poppy. She's feeling –"

I cut her off. "She should," I said. "She should feel bad, or abandoned, or whatever the hell she's feeling." It felt good to say those words, but in the next instant something in Calypso's face made me feel even worse than I already did. I sat up, pushing the quilt away, so that it half slid off the bed.

"This isn't about Mom. It's about this person I've been spending time with," I said.

"Mac?" she asked, a smile playing around the edges of her mouth.

I shook my head, irritated. "No," I said. "I'm not talking about Mac. It's someone else."

Her smile wasn't quite as bright. "Do you want some lemon balm and chamomile tea? It's very calming. Or I could get Eric to run out and pick up some skullcap tablets. Skullcap helps with anxiety."

I shook my head. "Remember when we were talking before, and I said maybe I would meet my real mother on the street?"

Calypso nodded, and what was left of her smile dropped away like a two-day-old bandage.

"Well," I said, my voice getting louder. "I did. I have." My chin felt rubbery.

"Okay," she said, something like a frown around her eyes, "just tell me what happened."

So I told her. About first meeting Becca, and Sandeep going into her house, and everything I could remember – the stuff about the tree, and Rakel, and Nigel, and what Becca had said about the baby who she gave up for adoption. Her daughter. And the similarities between us. And that the similarities were more than that. They were certainties.

"She's my mother, Calypso," I said. "It's really her."

Calypso sat there quietly, picking at a loose thread on the quilt.

"I have something to confess, Poppy," she finally said.

I waited.

"When you asked me about my father, I told you that I didn't care about finding him. That it didn't matter."

"Yeah. And?"

"I lied. I thought about him all the time when I was

growing up. Even after I was an adult. I carried a really clear picture of him in my head, from the way my mother described him. For a long time he was eighteen in my head picture, the age he was when he and my mother met. But then I started to let him grow older."

"Yeah?" *What does this have to do with Becca? Or with me?*

Calypso pulled harder at the thread. "The picture I had of him was a man of medium height. Slim. Curly, dark blond hair, still long, like my mother said it was at Woodstock, even though I knew there'd be less of it. Blue eyes that crinkle up when he smiles – a wide smile. That's the picture I had in my head."

I frowned. "But Calypso, that sounds like –"

"Of course." The uneasy look had disappeared from her face. "Of course," she said again. "It's just like Eric. And from the minute I saw him – your dad – singing 'These Boots Are Made For Walking' as the opening act at Sea World in San Diego, I wanted to be near him. I didn't realize why, at the time. He just looked like somebody . . ." she paused, looking for the right word ". . . safe. He looked safe. And when I got to know him, he made me feel safe."

"You fell in love with him because he looked like your own father?" I made a gagging sound.

"The point is, Poppy, I was looking, too, looking for my father everywhere, although I didn't realize it at the time. I just liked the way Eric looked and, when I got to know him, I fell in love with him. I don't feel like he *is* my father or anything. But I was drawn to him, at first, because I *wanted* to be drawn to him."

"So you're saying that's what I'm doing with Becca? Imagining all these coincidences, imagining that she could be my mother because I want to find my real mother?"

Calypso looked up from the bed, into my eyes. "Only you can answer that, Poppy."

"Basically you're saying you don't believe me."

"Do you really think she is? I mean, that's sort of movie material, isn't it?" She brushed a piece of hair away from my face, tucking it behind my ear like I'd seen Rakel do to Becca.

I wanted to lay my cheek against her hand. My eyes filled with tears again, and I squeezed them shut, hating that I was feeling so weak.

"I think you should try and go back to sleep. Things will look better in the morning," Calypso said, like Dad had said to me last night. Her mouth was a wavy line that looked like a cross between a smile and a frown. She straightened the quilt and turned out my lamp.

You'll see, Calypso. I watched her leave, both her hands pressed to the small of her back. *You'll all see. Calypso, and Dad, and Mac. You'll see that Becca really is my mother. I'll prove it.*

Tomorrow.

TWENTY

The next day was cool and windy. I hadn't really slept much; I knew what I had to do, and I'd spent a lot of the long dark hours thinking about what I'd say to Becca.

Calypso had a bad morning; she stayed in bed, saying she hadn't felt right all night, and could I watch Sandeep for just a few hours. I thought about taking him with me over to Palmerston, but almost immediately realized I couldn't even think of talking seriously to Becca with Sandeep around. Instead I took him to Vimy Ridge Park, then colored with him and gave him lunch. Still Calypso didn't come down. I played with Sandeep some more, helping him with his huge Lego pieces, got him to have a nap, and eventually gave him supper. Dad phoned to say he was working a couple of extra hours. I glanced at my watch every few minutes.

Calypso finally came downstairs, her hair unbraided and matted against the back of her head, her eyes dull.

"I have to go out, Calypso," I said. "Sandeep's fine; he's had supper and now he's watching a Muppet video. Okay? I'm going now."

Calypso fluttered her hand at me, nodding. "Did your dad phone?"

"Yeah," I said. "He'll be home about seven."

I ran out and hopped on my bike. It was hard cycling against the wind, and I wished I had put on a sweatshirt. The wind blew right through my thin shirt. I was aware of being cold, but it didn't matter.

The trees were full again. I hadn't noticed it happening, the trees repairing themselves after the worm pillage, but today they looked a lot better than they had when I'd arrived.

As I drove up to Becca's, Mac was just going up the steps of his house, wearing his goofy safari outfit.

"Hey," he called.

"Hi," I said, waving, but not wanting to stop. I didn't want to lose my focus, the reason I was going to see Becca.

Leaving my bike lying in the front yard, I rang the bell. No answer. I rang it again, then tried the knob. It was locked.

I can't stand this. I have to see her.

I went to the side door, thinking that maybe she or Rakel were in the kitchen, but before I tried that door I heard big, painful-sounding hacking coughs from the backyard.

Looking into the backyard, the first thing I saw was a doll carriage near the elm tree. And then I saw Becca, on a blanket under the tree. She was wearing her house-coat again, but she had a thick white sweater over it.

She also had on white socks, and a pair of fuzzy mauve slippers. Her hair, for the first time since I'd met her, looked unbrushed.

When she saw me standing at the back of the house, she waved and threw me a little kiss, then held one finger to her lips, pointing to the carriage.

My heart was thumping in tandem with each of my footsteps as I walked toward her. When I got closer, I saw that the doll carriage was very old. The bottom was tin, cream-colored, with a thin line of green running along the sides. The top, which was up, was black leather, all crackly with white lines.

Becca motioned for me to come closer. She reached out and took my hand in hers. "Poppy," she said. That's all. Just my name. But the way she said it made the thumping of my heart almost unbearable. The skin of her hand felt papery, the bones like tiny twigs.

She pointed into the carriage, wanting me to look inside. But I didn't want to; I wanted to look at her – to study her features – the way she sat, the shape of her lips. Today they had a bluish tinge. I wanted to see everything, take all the little details and hold them close.

Finally I looked into the carriage. Blanche was sleeping on a folded towel. She was dressed in a little pink wool sweater. A darker pink ribbon was threaded around the top, and tied in a bow across Blanche's chest to keep it on. There was a matching pink bonnet on her head, loosely tied under her chin with satin ribbons. Her tiny ears poked up under the bonnet, giving the hat a strange, peaked look.

"Isn't she the sweetest thing you've ever seen?" Becca whispered.

I nodded.

"I got my old doll carriage from the basement. Then I took some pictures of her," Becca went on, clearing her throat, her voice becoming a little louder now. She picked up a camera from beside her on the blanket, her hands trembly. "She's so willing. She sat still, nice as you please, while I dressed her up and took her picture. But all the excitement tired her out. She's asleep."

I just nodded again.

"When she wakes up, will you take a picture of the two of us? I want it for my album," Becca said. Her cheeks were flushed, and her eyes too bright.

"Sure," I said. "Are you feeling better? I came to see you a few days ago. Did Rakel tell you? She said you were sick. I was worried."

Becca looked back at the kitten, then at me. "I know you must think I'm ridiculous," she said. "Dressing Blanche."

"No. No, it's cute." I didn't want to talk about the kitten.

"All right. She's waking up. Come on, little girl," she said, lifting Blanche tenderly and cradling the kitten against her shoulder.

I picked up the camera and tried to focus, but I felt shaky and uncoordinated. There were deep, bruised marks under Becca's eyes, and her shoulder blades stood out like the beginnings of wings under the housecoat and sweater.

"You're shivering," Becca said to the camera. "After you do this, come inside and I'll give you something warm to put on."

She turned slightly, so that I could see Blanche's face, and smiled, proudly, at the camera. But all of a sudden she gave another series of loud raspy coughs, and put her hand to her chest. "Go ahead," she said, "take it."

I pressed the button, and the camera clicked. "Now another one," Becca said.

I did as she told me, seeing Becca's frightening gauntness, the kitten masquerading as a baby, and behind them, the elm, Becca's tree, with its red plastic ribbon. Out of nowhere came the memory of what Mac had told me about the Greek hamadryads, the tree nymphs. They lived in their trees, Mac had said, and when the tree died, the nymph died.

I kept looking through the camera lens, even after I'd taken the second picture. I was shouting inside. *I know you're my mother, Becca. And you know it, too. Stop acting like everything is normal.*

"Okay. Now let's go and get you a sweater," she said, getting up and brushing off her housecoat. She put her hand out, against her tree, to steady herself.

"You haven't heard any more about your tree?" I asked, lowering the camera. "They haven't been back?"

"No," she said. "Every day I pray that it doesn't have Dutch elm disease." She looked up at the branches.

"The leaves look a little better," I said, although they didn't. Not really.

"Do you think so?" she asked, still looking up, squinting a little now. "I think they do, but maybe it's just because I want it so much."

She was still holding Blanche as she started toward the house. "Strange weather, isn't it? I bet we're in for a storm."

"Becca," I called from behind her. I wasn't taking a chance on running into Rakel.

She turned around. "Aren't you coming?"

"Is Rakel home?"

Becca shook her head. "No. She's out getting a few groceries. Why?"

"I think you know. We need to talk, and Rakel doesn't want me here."

"Oh, don't worry about her," Becca said.

We went into the living room, and Becca gave me Blanche to hold, saying, "There's a sweater in the foyer closet; I'll get it for you."

The kitten was swatting at the ribbons under her furry chin, then twisting around and biting at the sweater.

"Let's get this stuff off you," I said, and undressed her. Free of the clothes, she jumped off my lap, gave an impatient shake, then sat primly in a patch of fading evening sunlight on the rug, watching me with her slanted, mismatched eyes.

There was a small plastic bottle of white pills on the coffee table beside Becca's inhaler. A blanket was crumpled on the couch. The locked mother-of-pearl box was sitting in its usual place. It looked bigger and shinier and, as I stared at it, it seemed to pulsate.

I heard Becca coming in from the foyer. Her steps were slow, almost uncertain, and she paused a number of times. "Here. This will warm you up," she said, handing me a reddish-brown pullover sweater. I slid it on.

"That's a wonderful color on you," Becca said. She sat down and picked up her inhaler, taking one puff, then another, closing her eyes and laying back against the couch. "You have the best coloring – beautiful dark red hair and brown eyes." Her eyes were still closed.

She got up then, slowly going to a mirror over a bookcase and leaning forward, studying herself, just as I had done in the bathroom mirror last week. "Did you know that I have red hair, Poppy? Much like yours. I'm thinking of letting it go back to its natural color," she said, coming over and stopping in front of me. "Seeing how beautiful your hair is reminds me of mine. I don't know why I didn't like having red hair."

I was finding it hard to breathe properly — not just because I had to listen to Becca's own painful breathing, but because I couldn't stand the tension.

"Becca. Sit down. I need to ask you something. Something really important."

Becca tore her eyes, reluctantly I thought, away from my face. She seated herself on the couch, pushing aside the blanket, smoothing her housecoat over her knees, and then folding her hands in her lap. "Go ahead."

I sat on the coffee table in front of her. A slight frown creased her forehead. "Really, my dear. Do take a chair."

"No," I said. "I want you to listen, Becca. Really, really carefully."

The frown faded. "All right."

The room grew darker, the lowering sun completely hidden by clouds now. I licked my lips.

"We need to talk about the whole thing. Your daughter."

Becca's face became gray and pinched, and her pupils grew tiny, as if I'd lit a match in front of them. She put her hand to her chest, coughing and reaching for her inhaler. "I don't think it's a good idea for us to talk about it right now, Poppy."

"You have to," I said. "Please." I waited for a moment, then said it. "I know, Becca. I know."

Rakel's voice, so loud, so close to my head, made me jump up from the coffee table.

"What is it you think you know?" Rakel asked, plastic grocery bags dangling from one hand, and a set of keys from the other. She studied Becca's face. "I told you, Miss Becca, that you must not move around while I was gone. What is the girl doing here?"

Becca was using her inhaler, and didn't answer. Rakel set the bags and keys on the coffee table. "Come, come up to bed. If you don't take care, it could mean a trip to Emergency." She helped Becca to her feet. "And you," she said, her eyes narrowing, "go away. Go. I told you before not to come here anymore. Look what happens."

She knows too. The old witch. She knows, and she's jealous. She's jealous of me. I'll spoil her perfect little setup. Right now Becca has only her, and she likes it that way. She wants to keep Becca and me apart.

"What are you waiting for?" she asked. "Miss Becca goes to bed now."

"Becca?" I said.

"I'm sorry, Poppy," she whispered. "This isn't a good time. I'm sorry," she repeated, and, leaning against Rakel's supporting arm, the two of them went toward the stairs.

I was left alone in the living room. Alone with Blanche and the locked mother-of-pearl box.

Outside, there was a low rumble of distant thunder.

TWENTY-ONE

I went over to the glass cabinet and pulled the door open. Running my fingers along the top of the smooth mother-of-pearl box, I stopped at the small gold lock. I pulled down on it, but it stayed firm.

Looking over my shoulder, I took the box out of the cabinet, closing the glass door soundlessly. The box was heavier than I thought, and I suddenly realized that it would be hard to balance it under my arm and ride my bike home, especially with the rain that was now hitting the glass of the patio door.

Mac. I can go to his place.

I left through the patio door. The rain was already coming down hard as I crossed the backyard, passed the ribboned tree, and pushed through the bushes into Mac's yard. I ran in the front door and up the stairs and knocked, fast and loud.

"Can I come in?" I asked, when Mac opened the door. He was holding a wooden spoon in his hand.

"Sure." He stepped away from the door, looking at the box I was holding, tenderly but firmly, out in front of me. "I was just making something to eat. Linnea's out and Tanner is asleep. Do you want something?"

"No. Look, can you help me?"

"With what?"

I sort of pushed the box at him. "With this. Do you have something, like a pair of pliers, to break this lock?"

He picked up the lock. "Yeah. But why? What's in here?"

"That's just it. I'm not sure, but I know that this is the proof I need, the proof that Becca is my mother."

"This is her box?"

"Yeah."

"How come you have it?"

I made an impatient sound with my tongue. "I took it, okay. I just have to get it open."

"You took it? Like stole it?"

"Look, are you going to help me or not? If you aren't, fine, I'll take it home and open it there."

"I don't get it. Why didn't Becca open it for you?"

"Because. It's too complicated to explain right now. But I'm not going to wait any longer to show everyone – you and Dad and Calypso – that I'm right."

Mac touched the spoon to his lips, studying my face.

"So, will you help me or not? If you won't, I'll find out myself, and you can go back to your cooking and pretend that I never came here. Okay?" *Why was I so sure that he would understand?*

Mac stared at me for the next few seconds. "Okay. Hang on. I have some pliers." He went behind the screen that made his bedroom, and then called to me.

The thunder rumbled again, still far off, but a little louder, more persistent, and a sudden flash of lightening blazed.

Sitting on his bed and holding the box on his lap, Mac fiddled with the lock and pliers for a minute. "Turn on the light," he said.

"Can't you hurry up?" I asked, sharper than I meant to, turning on the lamp that sat on his bookshelf. In the next instant there was a snap, and the lock broke into two pieces.

I sat beside him.

"This might be a Pandora's box, Poppy," Mac said.

I was losing it. "I'm not in the mood for any more of your Greek mythology, Mac," I said, taking the box. I opened the lid, realizing that I was clenching my teeth as I stared into the box, biting down on my back molars so hard that they ached.

"What is it?" Mac asked, leaning over so his head was next to mine.

I looked up at him, releasing my teeth, then reached in. There was a small teddy bear on top of two packages, each folded in white tissue paper. I set the teddy bear on the bed, then opened the first package. It was a photo and a folded piece of newspaper. The small photo looked like it was taken around the same time as the one on Mr. Hartley's wall. Nigel and Becca, smiling, holding hands on the front step of Mr. Hartley's house.

"Nigel and Becca," I breathed. "My parents."

I unfolded the yellowed piece of paper, holding it so Mac could see it, too. It was a newspaper clipping about Nigel Hartley, saying that he'd been a gold medal winner awarded a scholarship to McGill. There was a picture of him, dark and smudged, on the old newsprint.

The next piece of folded tissue contained a tiny sweater, booties, and bonnet. They were white, and threaded through the top of the sweater and the tops of the booties was pink satin ribbon. Matching ribbon was sewn to the bonnet. It was the exact kind of sweater and bonnet, although a different color, that Becca had put on Blanche. As I picked up the sweater to look at it more closely, a picture and a tiny plastic hospital bracelet fell out of the woolen folds. The picture was creased, soft, as if it had been handled many, many times.

Mac and I looked at it together.

It was of a baby, one of those newborn photos that are taken in hospitals. The baby looked like any baby, the hair a goldy-red, fuzzy and wispy. The eyes were squeezed shut.

"That's you?" Mac said.

"Yeah. Look at the red hair." I tried to think what I looked like in the albums of me as a baby that Mom had filled.

Mac took it out of my hand, studying it. "Yeah," he said. "It does sort of look like you."

I felt a surge of gratefulness. "I told you," I said. "Didn't I? I told you."

As I picked up the plastic hospital bracelet, Mac turned the picture over.

"Poppy," he said. "Maybe you should look at this. He held the picture toward me, and I looked down at the letters stamped across the back of it. HÔPITAL DE SACRÉ-CŒUR DE MONTRÉAL, it said.

It was like everything fluid drained out of my body. I was a mummy, petrified, my body looking the right shape but completely empty inside. I felt Mac gently take the hospital bracelet out of my hand.

"Hôpital de Sacré-Cœur de Montréal," he read. "Female. And here's the date."

I followed his finger, looking at the three numbers divided by slashes.

"That's older than you, Poppy," he finally said, after what felt like an hour. "That's like four years older than you."

I couldn't look at him. *Think. Be someone else. Who are you? Who can you be for this moment? But there's nobody here. Just me. Just Poppy.* I sat very still, studying the pattern of the quilted screen. *Why can't I pretend to be someone else when I'm around Mac?*

He touched my cheek. "Don't cry," he said.

I sat up straighter, the pattern of the quilt in front of me blurring into a kaleidoscope of tumbling shapes and colors.

After a few minutes, Mac folded everything back into the tissue nests and put them into the box, gently closing the lid.

"Do you want me to come with you? To put it back?" he asked.

"I don't need any help."

"I'll come with —"

"No!" I said, louder than I meant to. "No," I said again, quieter. "I can do this myself."

I didn't want him to be there when I confronted Becca.

TWENTY-TWO

I came in the same way as I'd left, through the patio door. I was soaked just coming from one house to the next. The storm was at its height, right over us, the thunder booming and lightening illuminating the sky at the same time.

The box was wet, too, the lock hanging broken on the clasp. I went through the foyer and up the stairs, straight to Becca's room, still holding the box out in front of me.

She was in bed, her body hardly making a rise under the smooth peach satin of the bedspread. Her eyes were closed, and her hands were folded on top of the blanket. The light from the lamp beside the bed bleached her face, and her breathing was horrible – loud and raspy.

"Becca," I said, my voice louder than her breathing. She moved her head a tiny bit, but her eyes stayed closed.

I touched her hand, and her eyes opened as if she hadn't really been asleep, and with difficulty she pulled herself into a sitting position. Her hair floated like fine strands of pale silk around her face.

"Poppy?" she said, the word coming out in a whispered stranger's voice. "What are you doing here?" Her eyes moved to the box in my hands. "What are you doing with my box? Give it to me." Her voice grew stronger, and she reached toward the box, trying to pull it out of my hands.

"No," I said. "No. First you have to tell me why you tricked me." I stepped away, yanking the box from her grasp.

"Tricked you? What are you talking about?" She pushed aside the blankets, putting her feet on the floor. She was wearing a long white nightgown. "I'm not well, Poppy. You know that. Why are you acting like this?" As well as her harsh, unfamiliar voice, I couldn't see anything in her eyes as she stared at me. Nothing.

I held the box in her direction, then pulled it back. "You made me believe . . ." I said, ". . . it was you. You made me believe it was true."

"What was true? Stop blubbering. I can't understand you."

"I'm *not* blubbering." I never blubber. "I'm trying to tell you something. You made me think that you were my mother. You gave away your daughter, and I came here, looking for my mother. Why did you keep telling me things? Things that made me think you were her, that you were my mother?"

She shook her head, reaching for her inhaler from the table beside the bed. She took three puffs, then reached under her pillow and pulled out a little silver bell. She rang it, the little dinger clanging, loud and insistent. "Rakel will come now," she said, "and make you give me my box. It's mine, with my things inside. My personal belongings. What right did you have to take it, and break into it?" She looked at the broken lock. "Maybe I want the past to stay where it is. In the past."

Rakel appeared, carrying a steaming mug. Her mouth dropped open at the sight of me. "What is this?" she demanded, setting the mug on the bedside table, and snatching the box out of my hands.

"Tell her to go, Rakel," Becca said, taking the box from her. "I'm too sick for all of this. She's bothering me, fussing about ridiculous things."

"She will go," Rakel said. "And she will take the cat." She went across the hall and opened a closed door, and Blanche slithered out. Rakel scooped her up. "It is because of this that Miss Becca is so ill," she said. "You bring her this dirty animal, and suddenly her asthma is worse than it has been in years. You stupid girl."

She thrust Blanche at me. I automatically put my hands around the kitten's warm body.

"Now go. Go away and never come here again. You have brought trouble."

I looked at Becca one more time. She was holding her box with one hand, the other on her chest. She was looking at Blanche, not at me.

"Go," Rakel said, giving me a push on the shoulder.

We were both totally saturated by the time we got home. I'd tried to shelter Blanche in the crook of my arm as best as I could, riding in the pouring rain, hardly able to see, my eyes blurry with the rain and with tears.

The raspberry house was in darkness when we got there, not even the porch light left on for me.

I went straight up to my room, stopping to get two towels from the bathroom, one for Blanche and one for me. After I'd dried Blanche as well as I could, I peeled off my wet jeans and T-shirt and, leaving them in a sodden pile on my floor, opened my closet to take a dry T-shirt from one of the clean piles. But there was nothing on the floor. All of my clothes were hanging up, neatly arranged on hangers.

I pulled on a T-shirt, then climbed into bed, holding the kitten against my chest, but she wouldn't settle down. She kept struggling to get away from me, sniffing and pushing at me with her nose, making funny little sad sounds. Maybe they were just her usual kitten mewing, but they sounded sad. When I let her go, she padded all over the quilt, up and down on my body, and then over my face and head. Her tiny feet felt like furry little kisses on my nose and forehead.

"Please, Blanche," I whispered, trying to cradle her against me, "go to sleep."

But it was useless. She kept roaming all over the bed, sniffing and mewing, even though I knew she needed to sleep. She reminded me of something, or somebody. After a few minutes it dawned on me. She was acting like Sandeep when he'd lost Didi.

I sat up. "Poor little Blanche," I whispered, rubbing a circle between her ears. "You miss Becca." I picked her up and buried my face in her warm pulsing side. "So do I."

I did feel an overwhelming emptiness, much worse than my usual gnawing spot.

Even with the cool rain beating straight down outside, my room was stuffy. Still holding Blanche, I went to the window and slid it up a few more inches. On my way back to the bed, I stepped over my wet clothes and then over another pile – the dirty laundry I had intended to wash that day. I knelt beside the clothes, Blanche still held against my chest. Rummaging through the pile with one hand, I found Becca's sweater, the one she had given me to wear. I picked it up and held it to my nose. It still smelled like Becca, the sweet flowery scent of her perfume trapped in the soft wool. It smelled like Becca, but there was something else. It smelled a little like I remember my mother smelling, when I was younger, and she'd sit on my bed when I was falling asleep. I don't think she wore perfume, but she had a smell, something warm and clean.

"Look what I have, Blanche," I whispered, putting the sweater against the kitten. She turned her face toward it, her whiskers twitching. I got back into bed, lying on my side with my back to the window, making a little nest of the sweater beside me. I put Blanche onto it. She immediately began pushing at the wool with her nose and paws, nudging and shoving and arranging the sweater until she had it the way she wanted it. Then she burrowed into the soft perfumed wool, her tiny chest heaving from all the digging and scratching she'd done to arrange her bed. She stared at me for a few minutes, as if she was waiting for me to say something.

"Go to sleep, Blanche," I said, rubbing my eyes with my palms. "Go nighty-night." It was what my mother had always said to me when I was little, and still said to me, as a joke, when she came to my bedroom to say good night. Even last year.

The little cat snuggled down, her nose under her front paws and her tail curled around her body so that she was a small compact ball. But she was still watching me. I could see the glow of her eyes in the dark, and before long I heard the faint but unmistakable rumbling sounds of purring.

My eyes were heavy and sore from so much crying. I rubbed them again, but it didn't help. Finally I closed them, and let more tears come, my arm around Blanche and the sweater. I cried over losing the mother I thought I had, and missing the one I did have.

TWENTY-THREE

I couldn't sleep. The storm had worn itself out quickly, the hard driving rain slowing to a soft, steady pulse. I sat up, listening to the rain and to the house, the absolute silence of the sleeping house, then took my *M* Book out of the bottom drawer of my dresser. In the darkness I ripped it up, page by page, fast, with loud tearing sounds.

Holding all the torn pages in my arms, I opened my door and stood in the doorway for a minute. It was as if the house were holding its breath; not a rustle, or a sigh.

Leaving Blanche still curled up on Becca's sweater, I went down to the kitchen, turning on the light and jamming the paper under a pile of junk mail in the recycling box by the back door. Then I opened the fridge and poured myself a glass of orange juice. As I stood at the sink, drinking, I noticed a piece of paper, folded in half and standing like a tiny tent on the kitchen table. It had my name on it.

"Had to take Calypso to hospital (Mis)," I read. It was a messy scrawl, written in a green crayon. "Come ASAP. Dad."

I dropped the note and squinted at the clock on the stove. It was eleven thirty. *When had they left?* I'd been home for at least an hour. *Why hadn't I come into the kitchen? Why hadn't I looked into their bedroom, or Sandeep's?*

I ran to the phone and called a taxi, then pounded up the stairs and pulled on a pair of pants. I jammed my feet into my sneakers, grabbed my wallet and, by the time I bounded back down the stairs, the cab was just pulling up in front of the house.

"Take me to the Misericordia," I panted.

The windshield wipers created a steady wish-wish, wish-wish, as we drove through the quiet streets. *Let her be all right.* Wish-wish. *Let her be all right.*

A receptionist at the front desk gave me directions to the labor ward, and I took the elevator up, the sense of dread growing. Calypso would never have agreed to go to the hospital unless it was really serious.

As soon as I stepped off the elevator, I could hear Sandeep crying. I ran toward the familiar sound, turning a corner to find Dad walking up and down a long hall, holding him. Sandeep was twisting in his arms, howling and hiccuping, Didi held tightly in one fist. When Dad saw me, his eyes closed.

"Poppy. Finally." He handed Sandeep to me. His little arms clasped my neck.

"I'm sorry, Dad. I just found the note. When I came home everything was dark, and I went straight to —"

"It's okay. Just take him home so I can be with Calypso." There were new lines around his mouth, and a small quiver switched on and off under his left eye. From open doorways in the hall there were voices and small cries and metal clangs. A nurse briskly walked out of one of the rooms.

"What happened? How is she? The baby isn't due for a few more weeks, is it?"

"They're prepping her for a Caesarean. I guess she'd been in labor all day. As soon as I got home, we called the midwife, who took one look and said Calypso had to come in to the hospital. Her blood pressure was way too high, and we thought Calypso would be safer here. We've waited for the last few hours, hoping she could deliver normally, but the baby isn't ready to come, and the doctor said it's too risky to wait any longer. To them both." He ran his hands over his head, pulling his hair back and looking up at the ceiling.

"Go home, Poppy. Poppy and Sandee and Didi go home," Sandeep said, putting his head on my shoulder, and then sticking his thumb in his mouth.

"The midwife's with her, but she needs me," Dad said. "I tried going in with Sandeep, but it scared him – all the machines and Calypso not herself. This isn't how she wanted it."

"I know, I know. I'm sorry, Dad. I'm sorry I wasn't there when you needed me."

Dad put his hand on my shoulder, gently patting it. "Okay. You get yourselves home. This'll turn out all right, Poppy. It will."

It sounded like he was convincing himself. The look on his face made me want to do something – hug him, or find some perfect comforting thing to say. But in the next instant he was gone, hurrying down the hall, his sneakers squeaking on the polished linoleum.

"Go home, Poppy," Sandeep said.

"Okay, Sandeep, okay. Let's go home."

We took another taxi back, and Sandeep was asleep in my arms by the time the cab had pulled out of the hospital drive. I lugged him upstairs, and he stirred and mumbled but didn't even wake when I took off his clothes and put him in a diaper and his pajamas. I walked to his crib, carrying him, but instead of putting him there, carried him into my room. Blanche was where I had left her, although Etta was beside her, her big yellow rump half on my pillow. The two cats lifted their heads simultaneously when we came in.

"Okay, Etta," I said, nudging her with my knee, "down you go." She jumped off the bed with sulky *mrrrow* and walked, slowly and arrogantly, to the pile of laundry on the floor. With an irritated twitching of her paws, she settled herself. I put Sandeep on the bed, then lifted Blanche, still in the sweater, and put her next to Etta.

Finally I got into bed beside Sandeep.

My closet door was open, and the last thing I saw before I closed my eyes were the shadowed gray shapes of my shirts and blouses and T-shirts, arranged so carefully on hangers by Calypso earlier in the day. Earlier, when she'd been in labor.

"Be all right, Calypso," I whispered, my mouth against Sandeep's soft fragrant curls. "Please."

TWENTY-FOUR

There was only a feeble morning light in my room when something woke me. I knew, by the dripping off the eaves, that it was still raining.

Looking at Sandeep, curled up in a deep sleep, his thumb in his mouth, I sat up.

Calypso.

Then I became aware of what had woken me. It was Dad, playing his guitar downstairs, softly. It wasn't the blues this time. I recognized the tune, although I hadn't heard it in years.

"Puff, the Magic Dragon," I whispered, in a croaky, thickened voice. Dad used to sing "Puff" to me when I couldn't sleep. I remembered now, remembered him sitting on the side of my bed, gently strumming, his voice low, smiling at me as he sang.

I waited until the song ended, then pulled Didi up over Sandeep's shoulders and went downstairs.

The phone rang just as Dad and Sandeep and I came in from the hospital.

It was Mac. "Are you . . . okay?" he asked.

I took a deep breath. "Sure," I said. "I'm fine."

"It's just that after last night . . . and I've been trying to call you for the last few hours."

"We were at the hospital, visiting Calypso. She had the baby. Another boy." Pan was adorable, his hair dark, eyes the shape of Calypso's, but he had the same little dent in his chin as Dad. They were both okay, although Calypso would have to stay in the hospital for close to a week.

"Good. That's good," he said. "Listen, Poppy, Becca wants to talk to you. She came over asking for your phone number, but I didn't want to give it to her. I told her I'd try to get in touch with you."

"Okay. I just have to check with Dad. I'll be looking after Sandeep while Calypso's in the hospital. Dad's not going back to work today, so I should be able to make it over there pretty soon."

"I'm glad you're doing okay." Something in his voice made me touch my mouth against the receiver.

"Can you come to Becca's with me?" I asked, softly.

"If you want me to."

"I do."

The rain had stopped and I walked over, not wanting to ride my bike. I felt too out of it, strange, a little uncoordinated from lack of sleep and everything that had happened, both at Becca's and at home. Signs of the rain were evident in the wide puddles along the curbs, in the fresh crisp green of the grass, in the clean smell of the air. And there was something else in the August air, some hint of good-bye, of summer growing weary.

I saw a man and a woman coming out of Becca's yard. They were both carrying clipboards.

"Are you tree people?" I asked.

"Yeah," the woman said.

"What about the tree in the backyard? The really big one that has the red ribbon? Does it have Dutch elm disease?"

The man shook his head. "No."

"So it's okay? It's not going to die?"

"No. And we're going to inject the roots to try and prevent the disease in the future."

"Good," I said. "That's really good."

The man and woman both nodded. "It's tough to lose the big old ones."

Mac must have been watching for me because he came out of his house as I walked up Becca's front step.

The door was open, and I called "Hello?"

"In the living room," I heard Becca say. Mac followed me, and we found Becca sitting in a chair across from the couch. The room was filled with light. Rakel wasn't in sight, but I heard a door closing upstairs.

Becca stood as we walked in. She had on a pair of beige pants and a long-sleeved blouse. The blouse was the color of the Aegean Sea, the water around the Greek islands, an almost unbelievable azure. I'd seen that color on the last postcard Mom had sent.

Becca's eyes were red-rimmed, the same as mine had been in the bathroom mirror this morning, and maybe because of the blue blouse, or the redness of her eyelids, or the sunlight on her face, her eyes looked incredibly blue. "Good morning, Poppy," she said.

When the silence stretched, long and sticky, I sat down on the couch, opposite her. Mac didn't sit beside me, but stood behind the couch. I could feel him close to me.

"Are you feeling better?" I finally asked.

"Yes. I'd been doing quite well, and even though I realized, very quickly, that I was having a reaction to Blanche, I wanted her so badly. I didn't want to believe being near to her could do that to me. Is she all right?" Becca asked.

"She had trouble settling down last night, but I gave her your sweater, the one you lent me, and then she was fine."

"I miss her terribly." Becca looked at the window. "Will you be able to keep her?"

I nodded. "We already have three cats in our house. One more won't hurt. And one of them has already made friends with Blanche."

Becca sighed. "It will probably be better for her there. Other cats to play with. Lots of people around."

"I'll get your sweater back to you," I said.

"No. Keep it for Blanche."

"Is that what you wanted to see me about, Becca? Blanche?" I asked.

Becca lowered herself into the chair, holding its arms as if her legs were too weak to support her. She ran a shaky hand across her lips. "Only partly. Mainly, I wanted to apologize," she said, putting her hand in her lap and looking up at me. "I'm sorry I was so rude to you yesterday." She licked her lips. "And I'm sorry that I led you on," Becca said. "I didn't mean to; I didn't have a clue what you . . . what was going on in your head."

I just nodded.

"My father was furious with me for being pregnant, and wouldn't let me stay here to have the baby. He still considered me his little girl, even though I had grown up. He was a very unforgiving man."

I thought of what Mr. Hartley had said, about Becca's father digging up all her rosebushes.

"I stayed with Nigel for the last few months of my pregnancy, and he was with me when I had her. We made the decision to give her up together. We were both too young, and just starting our lives. And we knew that we couldn't plan a future together; we wanted different things from life."

"But don't you want to know about your daughter?"
I asked. "Don't you care what's happened to her? What
kind of person she is?"

"Of course," Becca said. "My file is open. She can
contact me whenever she wants. As soon as she had her
eighteenth birthday I made sure my information was
available."

"And she hasn't contacted you?"

Becca shook her head. "Not yet. I hope that she
might, one day. But if she doesn't, I'll respect that. It's her
choice now. I made my choice twenty years ago."

I nodded again, blinking fast.

Becca was watching me. "I have to be honest, Poppy.
There was something about you that felt," she searched
for the word, "comfortable. Rakel saw that too, and she
didn't like it."

"Why?"

A warmth touched Becca's colorless lips. "She's just
overprotective. She thinks of me as her daughter. We
sort of cling to each other, Rakel and I. Each of us alone,
in our own way."

Becca remained silent for a few heartbeats. "You
looked for a missing mother. Rakel looked at me as the
child she never had. And I . . ." she stopped, and sighed,
an expression on her face that was almost gentle.
"Perhaps we're always looking, hoping to find the thing
we want — we think we need — in someone else."

I exhaled what was left of my breath, and felt a whisper of air stir my hair, as if Mac had moved his hand, reached toward me. But it passed.

Then Becca sat up straighter. "So, Poppy, I'd love to have you keep on visiting. Rakel will stay out of our way if I tell her to. Let's be friends."

There was that old eagerness in her face.

I thought of all of us — of Rakel, and Becca, of Calypso, and of my own mother, somewhere where the sun was a brilliant disk in a sky that matched the water below — all of us on our own personal quest, looking to fill an empty place. Our own odyssey.

"I think it would be better if I didn't come over anymore."

Becca's eyebrows raised. "But —"

"I'll be pretty busy," I said. "I have a new baby brother. And my stepmother and father are really depending on me."

"I could help you with your acting," Becca said. "I never got to show you all my photos, all my mementos."

"I don't think so," I said, and then there was nothing left to say, and the three of us were left in a hushed calm in the luminous room, the sun making its slow journey through the trees outside, creating patterns of leaf shadow on the ceiling and walls, shadows that rippled softly, soundlessly, over the room and Becca's face.

TWENTY-FIVE

Even though we're only into the third week of August, there's a different look to the leaves. They've lost the freshness of summer, and are darker, their greens heavier, older. Some are already turning gold around the edges. I watched the leaves from the top step of the porch, and the way the first sprinkles of rain bounced off them. Sandeep was playing with Blanche, rolling a little plastic ball up and down the porch for her to chase, when Mac appeared, carrying a small plastic bag.

"Thought you might like this," he said, handing it to me.

"Sit in here," I said, moving over on the step. "Out of the rain." I took a thick book out of the bag. *The Odyssey*.

"I wrote something in it," he said. "But you can look at it later."

"Can't I see now?"

Mac reached out and stroked Blanche, who had sidled up against him. "She's getting big. Yeah, I guess so, if you want." He picked Blanche up, studying her.

TO POPPY, I read. CLEAR SAILING SHALL YOU HAVE NOW, HOMEWARD NOW, HOWEVER PAINFUL ALL THE PAST. MAC.

I couldn't think of anything to say, and I guess I looked all weird, because Mac set Blanche down and put his arm around my shoulders, and I leaned my head against him.

"It's a quote from *The Odyssey*, when Odysseus sets out on the final leg of his journey," he said, his voice close to my ear.

Sandeep ran up and wrapped his arms around my neck, forcing Mac to move his arm. "My Poppy," he said, looking at Mac. "Not your Poppy. My Poppy."

I kissed Sandeep's cheek. "He's going through a territorial stage," I said, "because of the new b-a-b-y and everything." I pulled him around and set him on my lap. "Yes," I said. "I'm your Poppy. You remember Mac. He lives with Tanner."

Sandeep studied Mac's face. Then he looked back at me and nodded, one big nod. "Okay," he said.

Mac smiled. "You're a big boy. Almost as big as Tanner."

Sandeep nodded again. "Sandee a big boy. Go potty now."

I made the blowing sound he loves into his neck. "Yes, Sandeep. You're a big boy now."

"So when are you going?" Mac asked.

"Not for another week," I told him. "By then Calypso should be able to manage. But I'm coming back, at Thanksgiving, for four days."

He nodded. "So, do you like to write letters?"

"Letters? I'm a great letter writer," I answered, and we sat there, watching Sandeep and Blanche play together, until the rain started coming down harder, and we all went inside to listen to some of Dad's records.

❦

A day after Calypso came home from the hospital, Dad came into my bedroom. Sandeep had just fallen asleep on my bed.

"Calypso and I have been talking," he said, "and I made a few phone calls. There's something called a nonspecific search that I can do for you, in terms of your birth mother. We can't do anything official, see if she registered or start an active search, until you're eighteen, but an adoptive parent can find out some general information – like education, religion, if there were any brothers or sisters, things like that. Would you like me to?"

I thought of the torn pages of my *M* Book, still buried in the recycling box.

"It could give you something to think about, at least for the next two years," Dad said, when I didn't answer.

I went and sat down beside Sandeep.

"No. Thanks anyway, Dad."

"Okay." Dad looked at Sandeep. "There's going to be an empty spot in that little guy's life when you're gone," he said, going toward the door. Just before he went out, he said, "We're all going to miss you, Poppy."

I watched Sandeep for a while, seeing how his long dark eyelashes rested on his cheeks, and thinking of what it felt like to hold Pan. Ever since Pan had been born, I'd been so busy – with Sandeep, and helping Dad around the house, and then helping Calypso when she came home – that I realized I hadn't thought about my own empty spot. I looked for it, putting my hand on my stomach and sort of pressing, almost like trying to locate a bruise you used to have, touching carefully, at first, in case it's still tender, and then harder and harder.

I couldn't find it.

❦

After Mac left I read over the last paragraph of Mom's letter, the one I'd received yesterday, the last one she wrote from Greece. She had met some up-and-coming actress after a performance she and Marcus had gone to in Athens. "So when I told her that my daughter was an actress, too, she gave me an autograph for you. I'm keeping it safe. I'll be back in Vancouver by the time you get this. We're flying home tomorrow."

It was signed "Love always, Mom" the old way, with the *o* in Mom a little heart. And there was a P.S.

"I can't believe how many tall girls with red hair I keep seeing in Greece. On buses, on beaches, walking down the street. They seem to be everywhere. And I always think of you."

She didn't give up easily, I'll give her that. All those letters she sent, and I had never answered one.

I sat on my bed, listening to the rain in Winnipeg, and thinking about my mother in Vancouver.

Is it raining there, too? And is she listening to the rain and thinking about me?

"Poppy?" It was Calypso, calling up the stairs.

I went and leaned over the railing.

Calypso had Pan strapped to her chest in a baby carrier. "Your mom's on the phone, calling from Vancouver," she said. "Are you going to talk to her?"

I came down the stairs, stepping over Muddy and T-Bone. "Thanks," I said to Calypso, and went into the kitchen. Sandeep was at the table, wearing a striped shirt and a cute pair of overalls, and feeding bits of pita to Blanche and Etta. Dad was playing his guitar, softly, in the living room, and something spicy and delicious-smelling bubbled on the stove. I picked up the phone receiver.

Outside, the rain continued to drum against the windows of the raspberry house, beating in quiet rhythm to the familiar, bluesy strumming in the room next door.

"Mom?" I said. "Hi. I was just thinking about you."

ALSO BY LINDA HOLEMAN

Promise Song

The year is 1900, and like many thousands of children before them, fourteen-year-old Rosetta and her small sister, Flora, have been sent across the sea from an English orphanage to make their home in a new country. But when they arrive, their dream of a family vanishes. Instead, Rosetta faces greater hardships than she ever imagined – and greater rewards – as she learns the true meaning of sisterhood.

". . . Rosetta's pluck and determination make her an admirable heroine, and the story is exciting."

– *School Library Journal*

Selected for the 1998 BOOKS FOR THE TEEN AGE by the New York Public Library.

Mercy's Birds

Mercy's life is spinning out of control. Her mother seems to be shrinking as she retreats more and more to the security of her bedroom. Her aunt is growing larger as she retreats into tarot cards and alcohol. While Mercy tries to keep up at school and with her job, she lives in fear of the day that Barry, her aunt's boyfriend, comes back to live with them all. Will help for the family come from an unexpected source? And will it be accepted?

"Eloquent and impacting, Mercy's story is an engrossing one, charged with emotional depth."

— Booklist

Selected for the 1999 BOOKS FOR THE TEEN AGE by the New York Public Library.